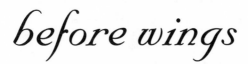

before wings

a novel by

Beth Goobie

ORCA BOOK PUBLISHERS

Canadian Cataloguing in Publication Data
Goobie, Beth, 1959-
Before wings

ISBN 1-55143-161-0 (bound) — ISBN 1-55143-163-7 (pbk.)

1. Title.
PS58563.O8326B43 2000   jC813'.54   C00-910773-8   PZ7.G597B43 2000

First published in the United States, 2001

Library of Congress Catalog Card Number: 00-105582

Orca Book Publishers gratefully acknowledges the support for our publishing
programs provided by the following agencies: The Government of Canada
through the Book Publishing Industry Development Program (BPIDP), The
Canada Council for the Arts, and the British Columbia Arts Council.

The author gratefully acknowledges the combined Saskatchewan Arts Board
and Canada Council writing grant as well as the Joseph S. Stauffer Award
that funded the writing of this book. She would also like to thank Dr. Iris
McKeown, Bill Martin, and especially Bob Tyrrell, for their contributions
to this manuscript.

Cover design by Christine Toller
Cover photos from www.eyewire.com
Printed and bound in Canada

IN CANADA: IN THE UNITED STATES:
Orca Book Publishers   **Orca Book Publishers**
PO Box 5626, Station B   PO Box 468
Victoria, BC Canada   Custer, WA USA
V8R 6S4   98240-0468

02 01 00 • 5 4 3 2 1

for Vince

part one

one

The spirits had brought a cold gray day. Adrien watched them hover above the lake, curling in and out of themselves with the wind. Female and young, they were sending their breath across the water in mournful blasts, kicking up whitecaps, dashing spray on the rocks, calling storms. These spirits still wanted to kick ass even though they were long dead. Adrien gave them a grim thumbs up and they wailed in return, their bodies twisting into the shrill notes of their voices. She could almost make out words, the same phrase called over and over, their smoky bodies shifting with each syllable.

"You'll get soaked." A maternal yank hauled Adrien back as a large wave came in with a crash. "Geezzzus," hissed her mother, pulling her soaked sweatshirt out from herself. "C'mon, let's get you into dry clothes before you see us off."

"Mom, I'm fifteen!"

"All daydreamers are two years old while they're dreaming." Her mother turned to follow the path that led up from the beach, stepping into the sudden lift of insect wings.

"Ugh," yelped Adrien, flapping at the bugs. They were everywhere, flitting through the camp grounds and along the beach, piles of their pale bodies rotting on the sand. The zillions that were still alive rose in a swarm of translucent wings with every step she took, settling all over her. When she pulled them off, there was a slight suction that made her think of leeches, and she waved her arms wildly as she followed her mother up the steep ridge and away from the beach. Ahead stretched a wide grassy area that led to the dining hall, office and parking lot. A potential bug lurked on every blade of grass. As they crossed the lawn, the ground was a continual explosion of silent wings, the air filled with flight.

"What were you watching?" her mother asked casually.

Ever since Adrien could remember, her mother had been casually trying to get inside her head. Her mother loved her very very much. Adrien felt that love closing in and fought on dim short wings to fly free. "Just the weather."

"Just the outer galaxies?"

"Something closer."

Her father leaned against the car, talking to his sister. As Adrien approached, his voice called out with a forced cheeriness. "Fell into the lake already, I see. And took your mother for a swim."

"Got an extra sweatshirt, Erin?" asked Adrien's mother.

"Will I get it back?" Aunt Erin demanded.

"Would I want to keep it?" Adrien's mother dressed urban; Aunt Erin dressed second-hand rural. Still quibbling, the two of them headed for the master cabin where Aunt Erin slept, plotting the next day's camp schedule in her dreams.

Adrien's father rumpled her hair. "Water's wet today, huh?"

"Yeah, wet."

"You're carrying a few travelers." He picked several bugs off her shoulders. Glancing down, Adrien saw she was covered.

"Yuck! What're these things?" She swiped at them, but the bugs had to be pulled off, one by one. Released, they fluttered a short distance and sank into the grass.

"Mayflies," said her father.

"*May*flies? But it's late June."

"Americans get them in May, so that's what they're called. Warm weather comes later to us frozen icebound Canadian Prairie types, and so do bugs. Mayflies last a couple of weeks and then they're gone."

"You mean I'm going to have to wear bugs for two weeks?"

"Then the mosquitoes hit full force," said her father, a smile floating over his serious tone. "You sure you want to stay here all summer? Your aunt's an iron woman. I wouldn't want her for my boss. Older sister was bad enough."

Adrien shrugged. "I can always come home."

Her father winced at her lack of enthusiasm. She

sneezed and he took off his red lumber jacket, wrapping it around her. "Last thing we need is you getting sick on your first day."

"So I come home in a coffin," Adrien muttered softly, but her father caught it. A whiplash of pain crossed his face and she regretted saying it, knew he would replay the moment endlessly, trying to figure out what he could have said to inspire her, change her, turn her life around.

"I'll be fine, Dad." She leaned into him and he hugged her tightly. This one brief moment was something she could give him, solid in the warm circle of his arms, while the wind moaned through the overhead spruce and spirits wailed across the lake.

"I know you will," he said into her hair.

They waited in silence until her mother returned, wearing a thin ratty Camp Lakeshore sweatshirt with multiple paint stains and a ripped elbow.

"I want that back," Aunt Erin insisted, following her. "I'm comfortable in it."

"I bet you've been wearing this since the Tories were wiped out."

"Longer. Since we repatriated the Constitution."

The adults laughed. There were hugs all around, penetrating teary looks from her mother.

"Keep the jacket," said her father.

"It's too big, Dad."

"Keep it anyway," he said, patting her shoulder. Then they were in the car, her father reversing, tooting the horn, while her mother waved furiously. Adrien listened to the sound of tires on gravel as the car disappeared around the bend. Every ten seconds, her father tooted the horn as the car made its way along the road that wound through the large wooded area surrounding the camp. It was a long road; they were holding onto her as long as they could. Finally, he sent out a chipper series of toots to let her know they had reached the gate and were passing through. Letting go. Gone.

The wind blew a dark song through the lift and fall of trees. The huge air was sharp-edged with the scent of spruce. Adrien turned to look at the lake. From here the spirits were indistinguishable, part of the bruised gray of water and sky.

"I hate these," she complained, pulling a mayfly off her arm.

"Don't bite," said her aunt. "Die off the first week of July."

Adrien shot her a quick glance.

"You'll catch your death in those wet clothes." Aunt Erin's pale blue eyes didn't blink. She had said the word and wasn't fumbling to take it back, cover it over, apologize. Maybe she had intended it. "Hot chocolate?"

"I'm *dying* for some." Adrien twisted the word, drawing it out.

"Bull," Aunt Erin said shortly, turning toward the kitchen.

Adrien took the thick white mug of hot chocolate and headed to the staff cabins to change into dry clothes. Though it had been Aunt Erin's suggestion, she was relieved to escape extended conversation. There was something about her aunt—thick, gnarled and pale—that reminded Adrien of a Group of Seven painting. The glacier. Or one of the tree stumps. It wasn't her aunt's face or the way she looked, it was the way she stood *within* trees, sky and wind. Aunt Erin sure fit into this place. Her first Camp Lakeshore job had been as a counselor when she was eighteen, and now she ran the camp. She had never married— Erin Wood made no place for small intimacies. Just looking at her, Adrien could tell her heart was a shoreline vast with water and sky, shifting shale and driftwood. Not a human in sight. Iron woman, like her father said.

The cabin smelled of wood and Lysol. Someone had opened the windows and cleaned the rooms in preparation for staff training. In two days, Camp Lakeshore would be invaded by teenagers and university students, hired as counselors, skills instructors and maintenance crew. Adrien would be working in the Tuck'n Tack shop at minimum wage, selling candy and T-shirts. The alternative was spending the summer in Saskatoon watching her father water the lawn while her mother propped up her tomato plants, all three of them waiting for The Big One to hit. Any time Adrien made a sudden movement, her parents would turn toward her, fear widening their eyes. Sometimes her mother moaned out loud.

Aunt Erin wouldn't follow her around like a worried sheep. She had made Adrien hot chocolate, then booted her out, saying she had things to do. "Sunday afternoon, grounds are quiet. Go out and explore. Supper's at five."

The cabin echoed Adrien's footsteps. Small shuffling

sounds crept along the walls. Birch and spruce crowded the windows, casting the room in a deep green light that shifted with the wind. She changed into dry sweats and a T-shirt, and draped her wet clothes over the other bed. The cabin had four bedrooms, each with two beds. She would have a roommate, someone else filling this quiet green space with loud talk and movement, conversation and judgment. Quickly, Adrien pulled on her father's lumber jacket and left the cabin.

She headed through the wooded area enclosing the staff cabins, then out onto the wide expanse of lawn with its frantic mayflies, toward the lake. A path led down a steep ridge to the beach. To her left was the dock; in front and to the right extended the yellow rope and buoys that marked the swimming area. Adrien climbed the lifeguard's chair and sat staring out. The spirits had gone down into the water and she could just make them out—shadows that rose and sank with the swelling waves. The sun emerged and painted the landscape with startling blues, browns and greens. Overhead, the shrill cries of gulls wheeled through brilliant clouds.

Her aneurysm had exploded out of a moment like this, a moment without expectations, a moment like any other. A similar sky had stretched without interruption into forever, the earth had run ahead of her feet, sure of itself, no widening cracks, no earthquakes, no tricks. Sure, there had been the headache, building for days, but who paid attention to headaches, even bad ones? They weren't as real as the grins of her friends, snapping their gum and making wisecracks as she stepped up to bat, the gym teacher winding up for the pitch. She had gotten it, had fought the massive pain in her head for that hit, could still remember the exact contained explosion as bat met ball, the sweet ache traveling her arms. The ball had soared into the blue like a heart, leaving her below within dizziness, pain and nausea. Still fighting, she had managed to take two steps, headed toward first base.

The second explosion had gone off inside her head, tiny sharp lights that swelled in a dizzying wave. There had been a sound to it, a thousand voices calling in one long note from some faraway place, and for a moment she had thought the light in her head was a bright hand reaching into her brain to scoop her up and take her home. Then the sensation of falling had taken over—falling into herself, arms and legs collapsing, bones and muscles meaning nothing as her face came down hard in the dirt.

She had been gone by the time she had eaten that dirt, had no memory of her friends' screaming, the gym teacher fending off their curiosity, the girl who had run to the office. Or the ambulance that had rammed itself over the curb and torn across the field to where she lay unconscious, having vomited and shit her pants. No one had told her any of this; she had reconstructed it from overheard conversations and some reading she had done on brain aneurysms once she had been let out of bed. That hadn't been for months, and then there had been rehab and home schooling. Much of it she had been too stupid, too dozed-out, to remember. Once she had gotten back enough of her brain, there wasn't much she wanted to recall. She was a year behind in school. Her friends had moved on, probably confusing her with someone who had died in a TV special.

It had taken her months to regain basic motor skills. Sometimes her brain would backfire and her legs give out; she would be eating dirt again. It was difficult to trust a body that had betrayed her so completely. Even now, she sat waiting for the one essential neuron to misfire, and her brain to go up in that final apocalyptic explosion of light. Rising, she would hear a thousand voices calling her to the faraway. *Dying, this is dying, wings of light, lifting upward out of—*

A rock flew by on her right and skipped twice before sinking. Adrien turned to see a dark-haired boy her own age sitting on the ridge, hunched in a blue lumber jacket and covered in a smattering of mayflies. Her eyes narrowed, but he didn't glance at her, so she turned back to the lake without speaking. Another rock flew by, and another.

"You're Erin's kid?"

"I'm not her kid."

"You look just like her."

Everyone said this. It was ridiculous. Adrien's eyes were hazel, her hair a long frizzy blond-brown. Her aunt's hair was wheat blond, straight and cut like a boy's.

"Yeah, like a truck looks like a Honda."

"Which one are you, the truck or the Honda?"

"I'm the one with the flat tires."

The boy's eyebrows lifted, then his face lapsed into moodiness and he threw more rocks. Adrien watched them soar and drop into the water. Down, down—she was being pulled down with the rocks, the day darkening, the air growing thick. Bubbles left her mouth, rising to where other people breathed, effortless and free.

"You're dying," said the boy.

It took a moment to clear the water from her brain. When she turned, the ridge was empty, the tall line of grass along its edge bending before the wind.

"There was a boy hanging around the lake this afternoon." The large room rounded and deepened Adrien's voice. Perched on a stool, she watched Aunt Erin make supper for two in a kitchen designed to feed hundreds. She supposed her aunt was pretty. She had the kind of face that drew eyes, but it was remote and alone like a profile carved into a rock cliff. Aunt Erin spoke to people out of necessity, and then she was done with them.

"That'd be Paul Marchand. Lives near here. Does maintenance for me."

"He's weird."

Aunt Erin gave her a pale blue look. "Got a sixth sense. It's a burden and don't you forget it. Carries it well."

Adrien pushed out the words in raw heavy chunks. "He told me I was dying."

Aunt Erin stopped moving and stood with her head down. "Well, and isn't that what you're always telling people?" She reached for the salt.

Adrien flushed, her heart jerking unsteadily. "But I didn't tell him."

Aunt Erin pushed through another slight pause. "Probably picked up on your thoughts. The boy reads minds. Hardly have to speak to him some days, just knows what I want done. How many cobs of corn?" She lifted the lid off a pot of boiling water.

Without answering, Adrien pushed back her stool and went over to a window. Her heart was a dark door, slamming in the wind. She put out a finger to trace the coolness of the glass and felt nothing. Outside, rain fell steadily. "D'you think he's right?"

Aunt Erin closed the pot lid with a clank. "Like I said, picking up on your thoughts. Walk around in a storm cloud like you do, you broadcast loud and clear. Hamburgers are ready."

"I'm not hungry."

"Suit yourself." Aunt Erin pulled a stool to the main counter and began to eat in silence. Adrien's heart slowed. Rain slid every which way down the other side of the glass, collected in small pools.

"I think he's weird." She spoke emphatically. "I'm not talking to him."

"Don't have to talk to anyone you don't want."

Adrien sat down and picked up a hamburger. "I like cheeseburgers."

"Cheese is in the fridge."

Her mother would have *asked* if she wanted cheese. Sighing heavily, Adrien took a bite and began to chew.

The rain continued. After cleaning up, Aunt Erin asked if she wanted to walk to the corrals to see the horses, but Adrien headed for her cabin. She knew she was tired, but when she made her bed and lay down, exhaustion poured through her. There was something about the huge, windy, spruce-scented air of this place. At home, her parents main-

tained a cheerful static, quickly covering her comments
about death and doom as if her words were blood—when
she made a wisecrack about dying, she began hemorrhaging
and they had to staunch the flow, shut her up. *Shut her up.*
Sometimes she screamed, "I could die, you know, I could
die"—anything to cut through the loving crap. Silenced,
her parents would stare helplessly. Once she had yelled,
"Why don't you have another kid, just fucking conceive!"
Her mother's face had crumpled, her father had gone white,
but they hadn't said what they were thinking. *We want to
give you all our love until you're gone.*

It was Aunt Erin who had suggested Adrien work at Camp
Lakeshore for the summer. She had called her niece directly
and invited her. "Can't pay you much, won't be a millionaire.
Just working in the store, nothing too strenuous."

A few hours and it had been strenuous, all right. Some
weird boy telling her she was dying. Aunt Erin treating
her like a mental deficient. The wind moaning in the trees,
opening up places in the air, calling spirits.

Since her aneurysm, Adrien had seen spirits. Perhaps
her brain circuitry had altered, or the worlds had rearranged
themselves to give her a taste of the afterlife. She didn't see
them constantly, but there was often the hint of something
smudging the corner of a room, shifting behind a tree,
wailing across a lake. This didn't frighten her, just made it
difficult to focus on the here and now. It was like being
pulled in different directions. She was standing in a shadow
land between two worlds and was being asked to choose,
but didn't know how to take those steps toward the humans
reaching out to her, their voices calling, "Come, come." Their

smiles were too vivid. She kept fending them off.

Aunt Erin and the weird boy didn't play the game of life, pretending there was hope. Paul Marchand was right. She was dying. Maybe not at this very moment, but it would come. The blood vessels in her brain were weaker since the aneurysm—they could tear at any moment, rip the life out of her. Her body would drop, her spirit rise ... to do what? Float endlessly in a gray smudge through rooms, watching the living go on without her? Join that line of spirits howling across the lake? What was it they had been calling, over and over?

Adrien slipped on her raincoat and made her way toward the water, looking down to keep the wind out of her face. The mayflies had been grounded by the rain, and a cold aloneness spread out on all sides. Why had she come to this place where no one knew her, no one loved her? She was an aneurysm victim. Didn't Aunt Erin know she had to be careful not to get upset, not to exert herself, not to stress her blood vessels? Adrien reached the ridge and was about to follow the path down to the shore when she saw her aunt standing on the beach, unmoving, her hood down, yellow jacket flapping in the wind. Out on the lake, the spirits moved in a restless line, a gray glow that was easy to distinguish in the dark—the vague shapes of five girls moving in and out of themselves, grieving like smoke.

Aunt Erin was watching them. Unaware of her niece, she stood staring directly at the spirits. There was no doubt about it, they were as clear to her as they were to Adrien.

Abruptly, Aunt Erin turned and came up the path. Startled, Adrien stepped back. As she peaked the ridge,

Aunt Erin looked straight at her and Adrien saw her aunt's face split wide with sorrow. Without speaking, the woman passed by, walking across the lawn toward the dining hall, while Adrien stared after her, tasting her aunt's loneliness, a heavy salt in her throat.

two

She slept heavily, through dreams of heaving water and a night sky coiled with clouds. Formless voices called through slow chaos. When she woke, she was sweating, her scalp soaked, even though the cabin held an early morning coolness. The rain had stopped.

It took a few minutes to place the unfamiliar bed, the rough blankets, the pillow that smelled of closed-in places. The room danced with a rustling emerald light. For a brief moment, she was sure she had stepped through to one of her dreams, waking in another life where she could be free of wondering if something was about to tear open inside her head.

The snapping of branches brought her bolt upright. Suddenly Adrien realized she was alone in a cabin, and something was moving against the outer wall. Wrapping a blanket around herself, she crept to the window, but saw only the lift and toss of easy green trees. More sounds came from the cabin's other side. She slunk down the narrow hall and peeked into an empty bedroom. Something shadowed the window, and a face peered in.

"Close the window and I'll take out the screen," Paul said. "I'm washing windows."

"I was sleeping."

"Close the window," he repeated, holding up a squeegee.

"Close your own window." She turned to leave.

"I'll have to come in."

"Go do another cabin first."

"This is the last one."

"So wait *five* minutes while I get dressed. What time is it, anyway?"

"Eight-thirty."

"Most people start work at nine."

He retreated and she decided she had won. But what if he snuck around the cabin and watched through the window while she dressed? Or came inside? She locked the bedroom door and pulled down the blind before changing into jeans and a T-shirt. Then she washed her face, brushed her teeth and carefully combed her hair. Make the prophet of doom wait. When she finally emerged from the cabin, he was sitting on the front steps, smoking. As she stepped off the side of the small square porch into a flurry of mayflies, he turned to look at her, his face as expressionless as yesterday, except for his eyes.

"What?" she snapped, flushing.

He shrugged.

"Isn't it against the rules to smoke at Camp Lakeshore?"

He shrugged again.

She hesitated. "So, can I have one?"

He gave just the hint of a smile as he pulled a pack from his shirt pocket and tossed it to her. She missed and had to bend to pick it up. So what, she couldn't be expected to be an athlete these days. A yellow lighter was tucked into the left side. She lit and inhaled deeply. This was one thing she hadn't fully considered when she had agreed to come for the summer, but then she hadn't known about the no smoking rule until Aunt Erin sent the long list of *Rules for Staff*, one week after the phone call. Not that it mattered on an official level—she was underage and Aunt Erin was hardly likely to sell them to her at the Tuck'n Tack store—but none of the other staff would be carrying any for an easy bum. After thinking through all the ways she could get caught smuggling in a carton, Adrien had decided this would be the perfect opportunity to quit. Perfect as in no two ways about it.

"Thanks." She started picking mayflies off her T-shirt.

He returned the pack to his pocket. "Any time, Angel."

"My name's Adrien."

He looked directly at her. "I know."

The opportunity was wide open. She had been poking and prodding people for two years, looking for this moment, and here it was. She gulped air. "How come you said I was dying?"

His eyes didn't leave her face. "Aren't we all?"

She dragged on her cigarette. "Yeah, but I *am*. Did my aunt tell you?"

He dropped his stub and ground it out, then slid it under the porch. "Erin doesn't talk about people. She's good that way."

"So how'd you know?"

He linked his hands behind his head and stretched, cracking bones all over his body. "I've dreamt my own death a hundred different times. A hundred different ways. It never quite gets me; I always wake up just before." His eyes narrowed and he stared off. "It's always the same day, the same place, but each time it happens a different way."

"They can't all be right."

"No, but why always the same time and place? I figure I choose the way it gets me, that's all."

She forced a laugh. "You're nuts."

"Then why'd you ask me?"

They watched each other in the quiet morning air.

"You still haven't told me how you knew I was dying."

"Just a feeling." He picked up a bucket and turned to go.

"Hey," she called after him. "Can you tell when it's going to happen ... to me?"

He looked back at her. "It's not clear."

"So, when's your big date?"

"Want to watch?"

"Just wondering."

His face intensified. "You'll be there. I've seen it. Hide the butt, eh?" A silvery swarm of bugs rose as he pushed into the bush at the back of the cabin. She listened to the squeegee swish in the bucket, then drip as it rose. Paul swore.

She took one last drag at her cigarette, ground the butt and slid it under the porch.

"Hey Angel, would you *please* go inside and close the windows?"

Her lips twitched with the hint of a smile. Surrounded by sunlit bug wings, she followed the path through the trees toward the dining hall for breakfast.

Three women in polyester uniforms stood at the kitchen's main counter, opening large boxes of canned food. Their voices could be heard from the dining hall's main entrance, interrupting one another, breaking into volleys of laughter. No English. Adrien peered cautiously into the kitchen. They didn't look like aliens, just three middle-aged women, bulging at the sides and wearing orthopedic shoes. Hairnets and weird words.

One woman saw her and broke into English. "You're Adrien, right?"

Adrien smiled with relief.

"Such a pretty girl. Looks just like Erin, eh?"

The hairnets nodded enthusiastically.

"Um, could I have breakfast?" Adrien asked.

"Breakfast?" The first woman rolled her eyes dramatically. "Maybe you could show up before noon?"

"Just bread and water?" Adrien hedged.

The women whooped. Corn Flakes, milk and bread appeared and she ate, listening as they lapsed into their weird language. Why didn't they speak English if they understood it? She tried to guess what they were talking about. The old country? Their children? Husbands? Sex? Adrien almost laughed out loud. Maybe they were discussing their latest Pap smears. Cancer—did the hairnets ever think about death? From their whoops, giggles and snorts, it didn't sound like it. As Adrien finished her cereal, the first woman returned to English. "Just leave your dishes in the sink. We'll get them later."

"Um," Adrien asked, "where do you come from?"

The women gave each other sly smiles.

"Ah, she wants us to go back to where we come from," said one.

"Wants our jobs," said another. "Wants to work on her varicose veins."

"It's these lovely uniforms and hairnets," said the third. "Everyone wants to wear them."

"Tsk tsk tsk," said the first. "Finish your school, then worry about a job."

Adrien fled out among the trees where she stood, cheeks burning. Old hags. She didn't want their lousy jobs. For all she cared, they could cook pork and sausages in every lousy camp in the entire country. Rude—they were rude. She turned this way and that, kicking at roots and flailing at mayflies until her face cooled. God, did she want a cigarette. That's what she should do—learn how to ask for a cigarette in whatever gibberish those hags were speaking, and run that by them. She would show them. By the end of summer, she would be fluent in asking for drugs, needles, condoms and porn in *their* language. Every morning she would come up with something different. *Excuse me, but do you have the latest issue of* Playgirl? *I lent mine to the campers and they won't give it back.*

Aunt Erin was in the office. "Great," she said, looking

up from her desk as Adrien entered. "Today, you'll do inventory for the store. Count stuff." She grinned, but she looked tired, her eyes puffy. Last night's scene at the lake passed between them, a shadow of cold wind and rain. Frowning, Aunt Erin pressed the bridge of her nose, pushing at something in her head. Pushing it away. "Leave the mayflies outside," she said.

Adrien stepped out onto the porch. The bugs sat in a resting position, their wings folded together and pointed upward. They didn't struggle as she pulled them off, but there was always a slight suction, as if their little buggy feet were holding on for dear life. *Yuck*, she thought, watching each one flutter away. *Putrid. Barbaric. Go thou to thy doom.*

As she came back inside, a lawnmower started up. "On grass already," Aunt Erin said. "Boy's fast as ever."

Boxes labeled *T-shirts—Medium*, *Sweatshirts—Large* and *Buttons* were stacked along one wall. Adrien was more interested in the ones marked *Coffee Crisp* and *Smarties*.

"No eating the merchandise," Aunt Erin admonished, following her gaze. "I'll show you what to do."

"I can count."

"There's last summer's records, and records from over the winter. Schools come out for the day. Church groups and conferences rent the place. Need to make sure everything's in order. Glad you're here to do it."

A storage area at the back of the office held boxes stacked halfway to the ceiling. "Hope you like counting," Aunt Erin quipped, then led her outside and around the building to where an awning opened out of the north wall. During the summer months, Tuck'n Tack operated like a concession booth. Aunt Erin handed Adrien the key ring that unlocked the door, the cabinets and the large service window. "Lots of air conditioning," she said. "Here's the lever that lowers the awning."

She demonstrated and Adrien played with it, watching the blue-and-white striped canvas yawn outward, then shrink back in. Out, in, out, in.

"Easily entertained," observed her aunt. "Good to see." Before Adrien could protest, she continued. "When you're working in Tuck'n Tack, kids'll come by with their counselors. Every cabin's got its daily time slot." She made Adrien practice unlocking and locking everything, then showed her where to hang the key ring on the office wall. "How many summers were you here?"

"Five." Adrien had been booked for a sixth, but her brain had blown that June.

"Here's the books," said her aunt, ignoring yet another obvious opportunity for sympathy. She explained how to decipher the numbers and columns and returned to her desk. Adrien began to open boxes. There were zillions of T-shirts and sweatshirts, each with two sailboats and five tiny waves.

"These are ugly colors," she said.

"What?" Aunt Erin looked up from her desk.

"Kids don't like these colors."

"Blue, green and red?"

"They're all dark. You need neon. Lime green, laser lemon and hot pink. A bright blue. You'd sell a lot more."

"Thanks for the suggestion." Aunt Erin returned to her paperwork.

Heat slapped itself across Adrien's face. She stared at

her aunt's bent head, then said slowly, "Don't talk to me like that. I'm not slave labor."

"That's right. You can go home if you want." Aunt Erin didn't lift her head.

"Well, maybe I will."

"Phone's right here. Help yourself."

Silence pulsed between them.

"Why don't you like me?" Adrien asked in a small voice.

Aunt Erin sat very still, her head down. "Like has nothing to do with it," she said. "You're working at a job for pay. I tell you what to do and you do it. Don't order your boss around. May as well learn that from me, or it'll get harder for you later."

What later? Adrien almost asked, but the phone rang and Aunt Erin picked it up. "Camp Lakeshore," she said calmly, looking out the window.

Paul peered through the screen door. "Coffee break. Coming?"

She knew he meant smoke break and started to get up, but Aunt Erin covered the phone and said, "Just started. Give it another hour. Then you get ten minutes." She returned to the phone.

Paul's eyebrows floated upward. "I'll come back in an hour," he said and left.

After the phone call, Aunt Erin left the office without speaking. Rigid, Adrien sat staring at the box of medium-size, navy blue T-shirts she was counting. They were more than ugly, they were archaic. Camp Lakeshore's logo hadn't changed in over a decade, and the two toy sailboats and five dinky waves looked like something out of a kid's coloring book. Didn't Aunt Erin know she was competing with extraterrestrials and Marilyn Manson?

She got up and wandered around the office. It held the usual boring stuff—memo pads, staplers, a calendar with scenic trees, copies of summer scheduling. There were two wall clocks, one on the east wall and one on the west, catching the sun as it came up and went down. Aunt Erin had everything clocked, organized and filed into place except Adrien, and this niece wasn't going to fit into her aunt's neat schemes without a fight. Maybe she would just have her final aneurysm here and now, throw up and die all over her aunt's tidy desk. Wouldn't that throw a wrench into things? She could just imagine Aunt Erin discovering the body, checking for a pulse, calling Mom and Dad. There would be tears, profuse apologies. Adrien explored every possible angle of "I was such a lousy aunt, I killed her with my terrible attitude." It gave immense satisfaction for several minutes, then waned.

She fingered through a stack of papers on her aunt's desk and her hand shifted the mat, uncovering the corner of a small photograph. Idly, she slid out the picture and scanned it. A group of girls her own age grinned at the camera. They were all in swimsuits, as was their counselor, a young woman with wheat blond hair and pale blue eyes— Aunt Erin in a Speedo, holding a life jacket and grinning as if she hadn't a care in the world. Adrien couldn't believe how much they looked alike. There on Aunt Erin's face, she saw her own forehead, nose and mouth, ridged cheekbones and jutting chin. Two of the girls knelt behind her on a picnic table and draped adoring arms around her neck.

Two more had wrapped their arms around her waist. They must have been nuts.

Adrien slipped the photograph into her wallet. There was a lot of information in this picture and she wanted to study it. She would return it later. Maybe. *If* her aunt behaved herself and started treating her with respect. Adrien comforted herself with a Coffee Crisp and went back to counting last year's ugly unsold T-shirts.

In exactly one hour she was sitting on the porch steps, waiting for her cigarette. Aunt Erin was nowhere in sight and she had counted so many T-shirts that a myriad of ugly sailboats were floating through the dazzling waters of her brain. She heard the distant sound of the mower cut off, then approaching footsteps. Mayflies exploded in every direction as Paul came into view.

"C'mon, I know a place." He had shucked the lumber jacket. Already his tanned face was darker.

"I'm dying for one."

He gave a slow appreciative smile. "You didn't bring any?"

"I read the rules."

"Yeah, I'm glad I don't live on the grounds."

He turned onto a path that disappeared into a shimmering dance of leaves and bug wings. Adrien swore and waved wildly around her head. "I wouldn't do this for any other reason, y'know."

He turned and grinned back at her. "No?"

She rolled her eyes and looked away. This was the way she handled boys at school—smoked their cigarettes and sidestepped their comments and hands. When she was alone, she thought about the possibilities—thought about them a lot—but she never let them happen. There was something about touching, coming that close—she was sure all that heat would light up her brain like a Molotov cocktail.

"Erin not around?"

"We had a fight and she took off."

"Already?" He ducked through two spruce and she followed, emerging in a small clearing. More mayflies. A halo of wings settled onto Paul's hair and shoulders. "This is where they teach school kids to build lean-tos."

"We're going to build one and crawl in to smoke?"

He grinned again, scanning her face. Adrien rolled her eyes emphatically, realizing how she had set herself up. "Give me a smoke," she said, delicately picking wings off her shirt front. Fluttering on her breast. How embarrassing.

He pulled out the pack. "So, what did you fight about?"

Impatient, she shrugged. "I just told her she needed to sell T-shirts in better colors. She bit off my head."

He handed her a cigarette. "Doesn't sound like her."

"Yeah, well, I don't like her much."

"Why?" He lit her cigarette, then his own.

"She's bossy."

"She's the boss."

"I don't like being bossed." Adrien wandered to the edge of the clearing, watching bugs rise through shafts of sun that cut through the trees. How could air color itself like that, green shadows and gold streams of light? Even the bugs looked pretty out here. She pulled one off her throat and watched it flutter off.

"Tough city girl."

She turned to find him assessing her, eyes traveling slowly. "Stop that." She waved her hand, breaking his gaze, and he turned to look into the woods. "I'm not easy, if that's what you mean."

"No, Angel, nothing about you is easy."

"Stop calling me Angel. You want me to call you ..." She searched for an appropriate name. "Darth Vader?"

Unexpectedly, he laughed. "Darth Vader and Angel— that'd make a great team. Cover all the angles."

"Do you *always* think about death?"

"Do you?"

She paused, considering. "The possibility is always lurking."

"Isn't it for everyone?"

"Not like me."

"That makes two of us, eh?"

This time she assessed him, the broad face, thick eyebrows, wide mouth. His nose beaked slightly, his hair was shaggy, down to his collar. Lower than that she was not going to look now, but just wait until *his* back was turned.

"How old are you?" she asked.

"Sixteen this July. You?"

"November. So how d'you get your smokes?"

"There's always someone who'll sell to minors."

"Yeah." No matter how many signs were posted, teenagers found out who was open for business. "You do anything else?"

"Drugs?" He shot her a look. "I got enough shit happening in my head. You?"

"Someone spiked my pop at school once, but I've never done anything on my own."

"You want to?"

"It was too weird." She had been terrified at the sudden lights happening in her head, and had crawled into a bathroom corner to sweat it out. After that, she had never shared another can of pop. "What d'you think happens, y'know, when you die?"

"Pain," he said softly.

"Yeah, but I mean is there overwhelming darkness or do you go to a place of light?"

"I don't know. I never get to the actual moment of dying. All I see is another way it's gonna happen, coming straight at me."

"I think it's light," she said. "That's how it was for me the first time. I had a brain aneurysm two years ago. My whole head exploded with light."

"So, what was it like ... meeting God?"

She shook her head. "It wasn't God. More like a star dying in my brain. Y'know how they explode when they go out? It's like that—a huge explosion, nuclear bomb, the end of the world. Boom!" She snapped her fingers. "Lots of people walk around with a blood vessel bulging in their brain and they don't even know it. Sometimes you don't feel any symptoms. It just ruptures, and you drop dead."

He stood quietly on the other side of the clearing. "So that's the way it'll be for you, eh?"

She took a quick breath. "Yeah."

"At least you know how you're going," he said.

three

Late morning, the sky clouded over. Sharp gusts of wind kept slamming the screen door. Two core staff who worked year-round at the camp returned from a day off and stood bantering with Aunt Erin on the office porch as if they actually enjoyed her company. Adrien watched suspiciously, alert for any signs of suck-up or kiss-ass, but there didn't seem to be any. Brain slumming, she decided. In order to survive, no, *like* her aunt's tyrannical leadership, they had tossed mental efficiency out the window and reduced to low gear. Well, that didn't mean she had to. At noon, she recorded her current total of small ugly red sweatshirts, and stood. "I'm going for lunch."

"Be back at one," Aunt Erin said.

As if Adrien couldn't figure that out. She banged the screen door and ran heavily down the steps, then stood letting the wind hit her full in the face. From here she could see clear across the freshly cut lawn to the lake, which rolled and heaved under an approaching storm. Thunder rumbled faintly in a slate gray sky. An eerie fork of lightning flickered low to the water, and a small shiver of white echoed through the inside of Adrien's head. Again, lightning forked the entire horizon. It was like watching her own brain, the knife lines of electricity that sliced through its heavy mass. Calling, the sky was calling her into the gray pulp of its brain, the dazzle of its forked currents. *Come, we know you, come and be with us.*

Staff were heading to the dining hall. Someone shouted her name, but Adrien turned and ran across a lawn of translucent wings toward a sky that broke open, again and again, into fierce light. She was at the ridge, starting down the path, when she saw the spirits darting over the water's surface like dragonflies, twisting as if in agony. She could make out arms and legs, different hair lengths, even breasts, but their faces were shadowed. The spirits were moaning, a low sound that seemed to be calling the storm toward the beach, where Adrien came to a halt, pushing to stay erect in the wind. She was sure the spirits were calling something specific—a short phrase, several words, repeated like the lightning that snaked the sky. Another sheer burst of white, and Adrien stepped forward into the wild lake, the call of the spirit girls, the energy of their brains dying across sky. Into some understood sameness.

"Are you crazy?"

Someone was dragging her out of the water onto the beach. She pushed, trying to turn back toward the lake, and was shoved onto the sand. A heavy weight sat on her. She fought until the white light bled from her brain, leaving her crumpled and soaked, covered with sand. When she opened her eyes, there was only gray sky and Paul's face staring down at her. Mayflies crawled over them both.

"Get off me," she said.

"D'you know what happens if lightning strikes water while you're in it?"

"I said get off me."

"What were you doing?"

"Get the fuck off!" she yelled.

They stood slowly, fallen trees righting themselves, trunks split open and rotting. She was *so* tired. How was she supposed to explain this?

"Nice scenery," she said.

Lightning flickered again, illuminating the incredulous look on Paul's face. She turned and climbed the path up the ridge, heading through the endless flutter of wings toward her cabin for a change of clothes.

A bottom corner was wet, but otherwise the photograph was undamaged. Fortunately, she had tucked her wallet into the pocket of her dad's lumber jacket instead of her jeans. Adrien stood shivering in her underwear, staring at the smiling faces of her aunt and the eight girls grouped around her. The picture was at least two decades old. Were people happier then? The girls' grins seemed impossibly authentic, and each face held its happiness differently. She was sure she had never smiled like that, even before her aneurysm. Most teenagers needed group permission to laugh, and then it was a sharp loud sound that had a manufactured quality, but once she had heard a girl let loose a free sound so startling that Adrien had turned to stare. The girl had looked so ordinary—brown hair, glasses, pimply skin.

Rain poured steadily, the cabin roof and walls a shell of sound. The scent of spruce had sharpened and the air felt deeper, heavier. Hunger hit her in slow waves. How was she going to face Paul? Would he tell anyone? If only she had thought to sneak some Smarties, she wouldn't have to eat lunch with Aunt Erin and her fan club. Miserably she pulled on a sweater, dry jeans and a raincoat, and headed through the dripping trees to the dining hall.

Predictably, Paul and the two core staff were grouped around Aunt Erin at one of the tables reserved for skills and maintenance staff, while the rest of the dining hall sat empty. Adrien remembered staring at staff tables with a camper's awe, imagining every aspect of the archery instructor's romance with the lifeguard. Back then, staff had seemed like fallen angels—prone to sin, but presiding over Camp Lakeshore with heavy wings. She had never realized they were just older versions of herself. Now *she* would be sitting at one of those tables and some fifth-grade weenie would fall in love with her. The whole thing was an enormous scam. Adrien dragged a tray along the serving counter and received her dump of macaroni, lime Jell-O, cucumber salad and a glass of milk.

"You're lucky," remonstrated a hairnet, waving her

serving ladle. "We almost went back to where we came from, waiting for you to arrive."

A hot flush oozed across Adrien's face. Silently, she reached for a slice of bread.

"You're missing your smile," teased another hairnet. "But Paul here—he's always got a smile for those who feed him, doesn't he?"

Adrien glanced behind herself to see Paul handing his plate over the counter for seconds. Suddenly she was brushed with the memory of his weight pressing her down while lightning tore at the sky, but in this vision electricity shot into their mouths—they were breathing white fire. The image faded, leaving her open-mouthed, not sure if she had made a sound. The hairnets were still babbling about Paul's smile, but she had a feeling he had picked up on something. Maybe the electric current. Well, he better not misinterpret it—she wasn't a weenie camper anymore. Adrien picked up her tray and scuffed toward the chattering table. There was an empty space next to Aunt Erin where Paul obviously belonged, so she sat at the opposite end where things would be quieter, less subject to electric visions and unreasonable heartbeats.

Rain pounded the roof. Lightning laced the sky, followed almost immediately by thunder so loud it seemed to rise out of the ground. No one reacted. Aunt Erin made a comment and the core staff laughed. They looked married, as in recently. Adrien glanced at the woman's hands and noticed an engagement ring. No wonder they liked Aunt Erin—they were in a state of premarital bliss.

Paul slid his plate onto the table across from her. "Pass

my milk and cutlery," he called through yet another volley of laughter.

Faces turned in their direction, eyes flicked between them, an eyebrow lifted. "Getting a head start, Paul?" asked the groom-to-be, a tall skinny guy with a black cowboy hat.

Careful as a curler, Aunt Erin slid Paul's knife, fork and glass of milk down the middle of the table, then returned to her macaroni without giving her niece a glance. Adrien felt as if her face had been erased, as if she didn't exist, as if she had died. Suddenly she hated her aunt. The feeling was like two hands grabbing her stomach and twisting it.

"Are you Adrien?" The young woman with the engagement ring leaned closer. She was plump, with dark shoulder-length hair. "I'm Gwen and this is my fiancé, Guy. I remember when you were seven years old, building your first fire with tiny little twigs for your Campfire badge."

"Oh yeah." Adrien didn't like strangers remembering things about her that she couldn't remember herself. And Paul was watching her again. She could feel his sixth sense scanning the air for trouble. At the other end of the table, Aunt Erin stood abruptly.

"I'll be up at the corrals if anyone needs me. You all know what you're doing this afternoon."

It was an order, not a question. "Aye aye, boss," grinned Guy.

"Adrien, you keep on with inventory. I'll be back to check on things around three." As Aunt Erin picked up her tray and headed across the dining hall, her thin lanky body was suddenly cast in sharp relief by a bolt of lightning that lit every window. Everything was reduced to black and white. The hairnets gave a soundless cry, the mouths in their brilliantly lit faces opening simultaneously as thunder crashed down around them, then faded into a long stretched-out silence.

"Tree on fire!" Aunt Erin ran for the door as Paul and Guy erupted from their chairs.

"Which tree? Oh please, not the Wishing Tree," cried Gwen, going after them. Adrien grabbed her raincoat, jamming her arms into the sleeves as she passed through the doorway into midday darkness. Rain was coming down hard—whichever tree had caught fire wouldn't burn long. The deluge pounded her hood as she followed Gwen's form through the bush, and sure enough, when they reached the others, the tree was smoldering but there were no flames.

"It is the Wishing Tree," Gwen wailed.

A huge silver birch stood on a slight incline in a clearing. It had been split down the middle, and one half remained upright while the other lay on the ground, exposing the blackened gut. Slight whiffs of smoke rose delicately from the charred wood. Aunt Erin put a hand on the split trunk and stood silently in the pouring rain, not bothering to pull up her hood. Guy put his arm around Gwen and she leaned against him.

In the wet and dark, nothing moved except the memories in Adrien's head. Every summer she had spent here, her counselor had woken the cabin of girls in the middle of the night and taken them to see the Wishing Tree. It had always been a night full of moonlight, the Wishing Tree's silvery trunk rising before them like a glowing earth spirit, summoning them into the whispering promise of its leaves.

Every counselor held the ceremony differently—sometimes the girls stood in a circle, sometimes they found private places to sit and watch the tree, but at some point each one touched the tree's shimmering bark and made a wish. That was the magic of it—a girl gave the tree a touch of herself, and it touched her too. Adrien remembered sending something into the silver bark, and the cool green wish the tree had slipped back to her. Now, in the rain, she stepped forward to touch the tree again, send one last wish into its dying life, but as she touched the warm trunk Aunt Erin grabbed her hand and pulled it off.

"You've brought something with you, girl," she said fiercely, the lines of her face made harsher by the rain. "I don't know the meaning of it, but you be careful what you do here. You just be careful with what's mine."

Aunt Erin turned and headed into the trees, her yellow jacket floating in the dark. Lightning flashed and distant thunder rolled. Guy cleared his throat uncomfortably, Gwen patted the tree and made soothing noises, but Adrien stared after the disappearing jacket. The first shock of her aunt's words was gone and something new was growing inside her. It was true, she had brought something. The spirits on the lake, the storm, the split tree—in some way it all belonged to her. Far across the horizon, the last flicker of lightning danced through her brain, a promise of what was to come.

"Erin's upset. I'm sure she didn't mean that." Gwen's voice reached toward her, soft and comforting. Adrien looked at the others, meeting their eyes one by one. It was easy, she felt powerful, made of deep dark earth, wet whispering trees, huge sky. Gwen blinked, Guy cleared his throat. Only Paul met her eyes, steady, silent.

"Of course she did." Adrien turned and headed into the trees. She had lunch to eat and a lot of ugly T-shirts to count. After that, an entire summer stretched ahead of her. The earth contained her, the sky held her close, her sisters were kicking ass on the lake. She might live longer than this summer, she might not, but if The Big One got her here, she would die in a place that knew and claimed her as its own.

The evening air held the coolness that followed rain. Bird song ricocheted through the trees. Adrien stopped unpacking her suitcase and listened as cowboy boots stepped onto the small porch and the cabin's outer door opened.

"Adrien?" called a voice. "It's me."

Me about summed it up for Aunt Erin. Adrien stood without speaking and waited as the boots came down the hall. Her light was on and the door stood open. Anyone with a forty-watt brain could tell she was here. Her aunt stopped in the doorway, yellow jacket dripping onto the floor. Bug wings clung to the wet material, opening and closing. Adrien folded a sweatshirt and put it in a dresser drawer. It wasn't a Camp Lakeshore sweatshirt.

"Leave the mayflies outside," she said carefully.

"They'll leave with me when I go."

"They give me the creeps. You should spray pesticide to get rid of them."

"Part of the beauty of life." Her aunt raised an arm and looked at the scattering of pale bugs. "Laid as an egg in the water, live for two years in the lake, then get their full wings and fly for one or two days. Harmless, don't bite, don't even eat once they're flying. Just mate, spawn and die."

"Two years as an egg so they can fly for two days?" said Adrien. "What a waste."

"Spend two years dreaming in the water so they can make their two days in the air worth it. Each second is full of mystery, things you know nothing about. If we spent more time dreaming, maybe we'd have wings too." Aunt Erin studied the bugs on her arm as if they were her dearest friends. "Correct term for them is Ephemeroptera. Comes from the Greek word *ephemeros*. Greeks made up that word after seeing the way these creatures live. Admired their ephemeral nature." Her voice held an odd note, straining against something. She looked up and Adrien glanced away.

"Sorry about what I said this afternoon." Aunt Erin's voice was abrupt as ever. "Shouldn't have said it. Upset about the tree."

"The Wishing Tree," Adrien said softly, folding a T-shirt. It wasn't a Camp Lakeshore T-shirt.

"Tree's older than me. Older than the camp. Thousands of kids have wished upon it."

"Maybe it'll live."

"Lightning struck its heart. Won't last long." Her aunt shuffled her feet. She hadn't come into Tuck'n Tack that afternoon to check on Adrien, nor had she joined staff for supper. "Everything all right?"

"Yes." Adrien started pulling underwear out of her suitcase, all of it labeled with her name so laundry staff could identify and return it to her. Aunt Erin hesitated, then sat on the other bed.

"You know summer staff will arrive tomorrow for Training Session?"

"Yes."

"Your roommate was on staff last summer. She'll teach you the ropes. I expect you to participate in all staff training exercises. Good for you to know what goes on all over the camp. During Training Session, Tuck'n Tack is open from four to five daily for staff purchases. When the kids arrive, you start working full-time."

"Sure."

"You're here for a reason." Her aunt still hadn't looked directly at her. "Don't know why, just felt you needed to be here now. Something to do with you, something to do with the camp." She paused and rubbed her forehead. "Won't have much time for you. Camp gets real busy."

"I know."

"Just wanted you to know you're welcome. I invited you because I wanted you here."

"Sure," said Adrien carefully. If her aunt was going to try for tears and a hugging scene, Adrien was ready to shove her into eternity. Aunt Erin stood slowly, turned as if to go, then turned back. In the overlit room, the bones of her face seemed too large, like Inuit sculpture.

"Need to ask you this." Her pale blue eyes watched an invisible halo around her niece's head. "I'm missing something. A photograph."

Adrien swallowed, the movement hooking her throat.

"An old picture—me and some kids when I worked here as a counselor."

Adrien's hands were shaking. She hid them in her suitcase.

"It's important. Let me know if you find it."

"Sure." Adrien listened to her aunt's boots walk slowly down the hall. During the conversation, neither had looked directly at the other. Now, in the empty air, Adrien could hear every drip of water that fell from the restless trees.

four

Her new roommate arrived early the next morning. Adrien was still somewhere in sleep, floating in an emerald green ocean, ascending through light that streamed down from the surface. Weightless, suspended in light, she floated without body, history or parents that clung to her with a suffocating hope. There was just the light and the deep echoing sounds the green water made in her ears. Just the light ...

The cabin's outer door slammed. Adrien's eyes flew open as someone began dragging a heavy object down the hall, muttering loudly. A kick sent the bedroom door hard into the wall and a girl entered butt-first, pulling a duffel bag. A few steps into the room, she stumbled over a pair of loosely tossed jeans and looked up to find Adrien staring at her.

"Oh my god!" she cried, one hand going to her heart. "Don't scare me like that!"

"I'm not scaring you."

"Yes, you are," said the girl. "Lying in bed all quiet and sneaky."

"I was sleeping," said Adrien. "I'm a sneaky sleeper."

The girl gave her a suspicious look, then glanced around the room. "This place is a mess."

"Yes, it is." Adrien lay back and locked her hands behind her head, watching leaf shadows dance across the ceiling. She had to use the washroom like crazy, but she wasn't giving this girl the satisfaction of knowing it.

"Couldn't you at least have cleaned up before I got here?" the girl asked plaintively. She was several years older than Adrien and chubby, with carefully curled blond hair and delicate pink and blue makeup. She looked as if she should be working at Zellers.

"I was going to clean up when I *got up*," stressed Adrien.

"Well, *get up*." The girl grunted as she lugged the duffel bag, inch by inch, onto her bed.

Laundry staff, Adrien guessed, studying her. *On a brave day, arts and crafts.* She could just see this girl gluing colored macaroni onto glitter-painted cardboard.

"My name's Darcie." The girl began tugging savagely at the duffel bag's zipper. "This damn thing's stuck. It's my brother's, he uses it for hockey. It stunk so bad, I sprayed it with deodorant."

"That won't help. It's not an armpit."

"*Anyway*," stressed Darcie, ignoring Adrien's biological data, "it's too small, but Mom said I had to learn to live

Spartan. She teaches ancient history. I don't think she ever went to camp as a kid—probably read *The Iliad* instead. How's one duffel bag supposed to last me the whole summer? What did you pack your stuff in?"

"A suitcase," Adrien admitted.

"A suitcase." Darcie sighed. "I had to squish things very tiny, then get my brother and his friend to sit on it while I zipped it closed. Ta-da!" She pulled out a curling iron, waved it around and set it carefully on the dresser.

"What're you doing here this summer?" Adrien couldn't help the note of incredulity in her voice. Her roommate was a cross between Barbie Doll and the Pillsbury Doughboy. *Thank you, Aunt Erin.*

"I'm the archery instructor." Darcie said it with pride.

"You shoot arrows?" Adrien sat up.

"Good," said Darcie complacently. "You know the difference between arrows and bullets." She pulled out a Camp Lakeshore T-shirt, gave it a sniff and wailed, "It smells like *hockey*! I'm going to spend all summer smelling like my brother's jock strap."

"Maybe if you spray it with deodorant, Spart."

Darcie set down the T-shirt and gave her another suspicious look. "Okay," she said. "I can already tell we're like night and day. Your aunt obviously put us together to teach us a lesson."

"What kind of lesson?"

Darcie waved a vague hand. "Oh, about each other, probably. Humanity. The love of life. She likes to improve people."

"She probably thought you'd improve me," said Adrien

grudgingly. "She thinks I'm a bump on a log. A grouch from the swamp. Something that lives in your subconscious and never comes up."

Darcie grinned, then pulled out a makeup kit and started arranging bottles of nail polish and perfume on the dresser. "I always had the feeling she thought I was kind of flighty. Like she could never figure out how I learned to shoot. It doesn't go with my hairstyle."

"You really can shoot, eh?"

"Win every contest I enter."

"Way to go, Spart."

"Up and at 'em, Grouch."

All morning long, the parking lot was a bustle of cars as summer staff arrived. Adrien worked her first shift in Tuck'n Tack, selling Mars Bars and sweatshirts to harassed-looking parents, younger brothers and sisters, and new staff members anxious to become Camp Lakeshore look-alikes. Darcie didn't need to purchase anything—she already had a T-shirt in every available color.

"Dinky sailboats, Spart," Adrien had commented as her roommate donned the blue version.

"Evolve out of the swamp, Grouch," Darcie replied. "Learn social skills."

Social skills, thought Adrien, handing two red sweatshirts to a father of twins, *do not come in my size. Do the dead use social skills? Do the dying? Should I take lessons on how to die politely?*

"I'll take a medium blue sweatshirt and an Oh Henry!,"

said an obvious staff-to-be. Mustering her dying social skills, Adrien handed the staff socialite her new sweatshirt and candy bar, made change and got a smile ready for the next person in line. It was Paul.

"We don't sell smokes," she said. "Not even under the counter."

He tapped the pocket in his lumber jacket. "When's your break?"

"The *boss* hasn't told me."

"Probably won't get one. Busy day."

"I'm experiencing a major nic fit."

"Don't worry, I've got them when you need them. Give me a Nibs, will ya?"

"Not one of these wonderful T-shirts?" Adrien noticed he wasn't wearing the Camp Lakeshore logo.

"Got one at home," said Paul. "If I wear it here, I get mixed up. Too many people wearing the same thing and I can't remember who's me." He slid some change onto the counter. "Don't die before I do, eh?"

She handed him the red licorice. "The excitement here is killing me."

He grinned and was gone. She endured until noon, when Aunt Erin helped her close the awning and lock up Tuck'n Tack. Then they stood on the office porch, watching the last of the parents bid farewell to their offspring in the parking lot.

"Hey Grouch!" called a voice. "Give me a smile."

Startled, Adrien and her aunt turned to see Darcie holding a camera in front of her face. There was a click and she lowered it. "Well, you made a heroic effort, anyway," she grinned. "Last picture on my roll. I'll mail it off tomorrow."

As her roommate left, Adrien took a careful step away from Aunt Erin. She would never have allowed herself to be trapped in a photograph with her aunt if she had seen it coming. Aunt Erin stiffened slightly, then spoke in her usual clipped voice. "Pizza for lunch. Flo, Di and Jo always make a great pizza for first staff lunch. Camp Lakeshore tradition."

Adrien shrugged. Pizza was pizza. How could anyone non-Italian claim it as a tradition? She headed to the cabin to wash up, then ducked around it and ran toward the lake. It had been a long morning without breaks, and she had been waiting to find out if the spirits would show on a day like today, when the camp was full of people laughing, calling, coming and going.

The spirits were gone. The sky was a canvas of fresh blue paint and a strong wind blew steadily in her face, trying to brush away thoughts of gloom and death. But the sunny view in front of her felt completely wrong, just like the photograph of Aunt Erin and her cabin of girls looked true but was utterly false. The real Aunt Erin wasn't a smiling eighteen-year-old or everyone's favorite camp director, she was a woman who prowled the campground like something out of *Wuthering Heights*, terse, dour, locked into some inner secret. That secret hovered over everyone, tangible but unseen. What was most real about this place was hidden in a second mysterious Camp Lakeshore, one that surrounded Adrien like a fading dream. But whose dream was it?

Then she saw the five girl-shapes slip-sliding the waves, their glow barely visible in the sunlight. Adrien breathed out long and slow. So, they hadn't deserted her. No matter how many people crowded the beach and grounds, no matter how many of them wore Camp Lakeshore T-shirts, the true loneliness of this place would remain, a promise between the spirits and herself.

She turned and headed to the dining hall for pizza.

It didn't take her long to figure out she was the youngest staff member. Most of the people crowding the staff tables were in the eighteen-to-twenty-two range and knew each other from former summers. The jokes being told at her table were all loud and inside. Laughter rolled around like a bowling ball, knocking down everyone except her. Adrien ate in silence until a lull appeared, then lunged for it.

"The Wishing Tree was struck by lightning," she said, not looking up. "Last night."

"The ol' Wishing Tree, eh?" drawled the guy sitting across from her. He was wearing a red Camp Lakeshore T-shirt with cut-off sleeves and an expanded neck hole, and had mastered the art of keeping his biceps perpetually flexed. "Go up in flames?"

"Split in half," said Adrien, avoiding his eyes. They were too blue. She wondered if he wore colored contact lenses.

"Ooo," he murmured. "No more midnight wishes."

"Now we just have to figure out how to stop the midnight pee trips," sighed a girl in a University of Saskatchewan Huskies sweatshirt.

"Nothing to drink after high noon," said the guy. "On pain of death." The girls at the table seemed to find this

riotously funny. Adrien sat, absorbing this latest truth—
the Wishing Tree was another scam, perpetrated on weenies
hopeful enough to fall for it.

"But don't you think," she shot into the beginning of
yet another inside joke, "little kids need that sort of stuff?
Half the tree's alive—you can still use it."

Once again, the very blue eyes settled on her. This time,
she made herself stare back. The guy looked old enough to
be attending university, but he had streaked the top of his
hair platinum blond like someone searching for easy popu-
larity. He definitely looked manufactured. "Who are you?"
asked the guy in a careless voice. "An early camper?"

The Huskies girl tittered and slapped his arm lightly.
The guy had a ready-made fan club.

"Where'd you get that cute little T-shirt?" asked Adrien.
"The Jock-for-Brains shop?"

The blue eyes flickered in surprise, then hardened as
the guy tilted his chair onto its back legs and focused on
her. Suddenly Adrien realized her table was in the middle
of a long pause and no one was going to speak a word until
Jock-for-Brains did. She had stumbled onto some kind of
social elite and taken on the guy in charge. She chanced
another glance and found the blue eyes still studying her.
Everyone else had developed a manic fixation on their pizza.

"So, I asked you a question," the guy said finally. "Who
are you?"

"Adrien Wood." She stretched out the words so she
didn't sound too obedient.

"What're you doing here?"

"Tuck'n Tack. I sell T-shirts." She tasted the last phrase,

almost smiling. The guy let his chair drop forward and leaned forward, jaw jutting.

"We'll see how your summer goes for you, Adrien *Wood*." He stood abruptly and joined the serving line for more pizza. The conversation at the table gradually picked up, but no one spoke to her, and when Jock-for-Brains returned, he also ignored her. Well, that was all right. She hadn't been thrilled with the conversation anyway. To quote the hairnets, this was one guy who could go back to where he came from, and further.

The early afternoon was spent on an orienteering exercise that split everyone into small groups and sent them all over the grounds, picking mayflies off their bodies while they explored the camp layout. Adrien trailed along behind her group. Trying to give her niece a social edge, Aunt Erin had placed her with several new staff, but it had backfired miserably. The others were several years older and completely ignored her, so Adrien didn't offer any help solving clues. The group wandered perpetually in the wrong direction, up by the corrals when they should have been east of the Arts and Crafts building, close to the lake. As they straggled past, Adrien caught a glimpse of Paul working on the paddock fence. How come he didn't have to attend Training Session? It couldn't be due to his advanced social skills.

"Who's the cute guy?" asked one of the girls.

"The Doomsday Man," said a guy. "I heard about him. The guy's hooked on gloom—won't talk, won't smile, won't drink a beer. Lives around here somewhere and works on maintenance—cleans the cans."

"Too bad," said the girl. "I like his butt."

"Check mine out," said the guy, offering his, and the giggling girl swatted him. As the group rounded a bend in the trail, Adrien glanced back to see that Paul had straightened and was watching her. She stopped, caught in a beam of light descending through the trees, the wings of insects flickering gold-white about her. The distance made it too far for words, so it was just eyes, the two of them locked into a sudden staring silence that deepened until she could hear the slow pound of her heart. The trees sighed heavily, a horse wickered, the earth let loose a rich dizzying scent. There was the slight pressure of a mayfly on her wrist, the heat of her sunburnt lips, and then the memory from the beach—the weight of Paul's body, his hands pressing her shoulders, and something else—a scream rising through her so raw it threatened to tear open her face. But she hadn't screamed at the beach, she was sure she hadn't screamed. Adrien turned and stumbled after her group, clenching and unclenching her fists until her heart slowed, the scent of the earth receded, and the trees stopped giving their soft whispering sighs.

Her group came in last, having missed half their clues. Adrien ignored Aunt Erin's penetrating look. Everyone had gathered in the dining hall for an information session. Gwen and Guy were handing out booklets as Aunt Erin introduced the chain of command—the assistant director Maurice Turcotte and his wife, the nurse, and the hairnets, who smiled and bobbed through a standing ovation. When the applause quieted, Guy was introduced as coordinator of skills and maintenance staff, and Gwen as leader of the female counselors. Adrien stood dutifully to be introduced as Tuck'n Tack staff, but wasn't surprised at the dull looks she received. Then a series of shrill whistles pierced the air. She turned to see Paul, Gwen and Guy at the back of the room, the three of them leaning forward, their fingers between their lips. Adrien flushed and sat down quickly, but cheers of "Adri*en*, Adri*en*" began, Guy waving his hat, Paul and Gwen stomping and clapping. Another whistle blasted and Darcie waved at her from across the room.

"As you can see," said Aunt Erin, "my niece has developed her own fan club. Be good to her—she controls your daily sugar intake."

Everyone chuckled agreeably. Aunt Erin listed off the skills instructors, Darcie beaming like a low-level sun, Jock-for-Brains lifting a casual hand as he was introduced as Connor Evans, waterfront coordinator. The rest of the afternoon was spent going over the training manual. No smoking, no alcohol, no drugs, no sex in front of the campers ... Aunt Erin presented an admirable combo act of wry humor and tough lady. Adrien got the feeling everyone knew it would be better not to break Camp Lakeshore's morality code, or at least not get caught.

After supper, she hung around the evening campfire, but once again it was older staff and inside jokes. Even eighteen-year-old Darcie had better things to do than talk to a fifteen-year-old weenie. After a phone call home to let her parents know The Big One hadn't hit yet, Adrien headed to bed early. She half-woke when Darcie stumbled in at eleven-thirty. A few hours later, she woke a second time to find a flashlight shining in her face.

"Is this your first year on staff?" asked a voice. The flashlight began clicking on and off repeatedly.

"Huh?" Adrien was in a sleep stupor, the harsh light pulling her in and out of consciousness.

"Is this your first year on staff?" the voice demanded again.

"What is this?" She pushed herself up onto her elbows, then realized the idiot with the flashlight was a guy and ducked back under the covers, but they were pulled off. Shrinking into herself, she wrapped her arms around her knees.

"Get her some sweats and take her outside," said the guy, flashing the light at Darcie, who was sitting up in bed. The light returned to Adrien, resting full in her face. "Initiation night for new recruits. Be outside in five." The flashlight went off and several figures left the room. Adrien could hear Darcie moving around in the dark.

"C'mon," said her roommate. "I set these out for you. Put them on."

"What's going on?" Adrien didn't move. She had recognized that voice—it belonged to Jock-for-Brains, officially Connor Evans.

"It's just initiation. I went through it last year. No big deal."

"Maybe I don't want to be initiated." Adrien waited but Darcie didn't respond, so she asked hesitantly, "What do they do?"

"You'll see. Put these on. No, don't turn on the light."

"Why not?"

"It's part of the secrecy of the whole thing. The tradition."

"I don't like traditions."

"Look, Grouch," said Darcie. "Traditions are what make you part of a group. D'you want to be part of the group, or d'you want to be a reject?"

"I want," grumbled Adrien, "to go back to sleep."

But Darcie seemed to have survived her initiation. In fact, she had become quite a social success, so Adrien put on the sweatsuit and runners she was handed, then followed her roommate outside to where the rest of the cabin stood waiting. They set off without speaking into the woods, traveling away from the dining hall, the office and Aunt Erin's master cabin, on past the boys' cabins and the corrals, deep into a wooded area Adrien had never seen. The moon was clouded over, but the girl leading them had a small flashlight and was checking for strips of white cloth that had been tied to trees. Adrien thought they were moving in concentric circles, but when she pointed this out, she was immediately shushed.

After about twenty minutes, a light could be seen flickering through the trees. There were voices, the odd burst of laughter. Adrien smelled smoke. They emerged into a clearing and she saw a small fire in a ring of stones, a spot that had obviously been used many times. Why had she never seen this place? Off to one side was a stack of beer. Summer staff milled around drinking, laughing and talking in low voices. No one from the upper chain of command was present—not Gwen or Guy, the assistant director or the nurse. When the new arrivals were noticed, cans of beer were opened and handed to them. Remembering her experience at school, Adrien tried to hand hers back, but was refused.

"Free beer," a guy told her enthusiastically. "Part of initiation. Chug-a-lug."

Adrien pulled back into the crowd and set down her can. She felt safe enough—for once it was an advantage to be an unnoticed weenie—and the party's purpose seemed to be nothing more than breaking the no-drinking and no-smoking rules. Then Connor Evans stepped onto a tree stump and gave a short whistle. His voice cut into a sudden silence. "All new recruits step forward."

His platinum hair glowed eerily in the firelight. Adrien resented his tone of command, but joined the new staff standing close to the fire. There were sixteen of them, mostly guys, and they made up approximately one-third of the number present. *Why don't we just say no?* Adrien wondered. *There are too many of us to force into anything.* But the guy next to her was unsteady on his feet, and the smell of alcohol hung like a thick fog over everything. She was probably the only one who hadn't drunk at least one beer. This might have been a mistake.

"Welcome to your first summer at Camp Lakeshore."

A burst of guffaws greeted this announcement, followed by a wave of over-emphatic shushing.

"A long time ago," Connor began, "when you were all eensy-weensy little buggers in your beds, a tradition was started at Camp Lakeshore. This tradition has been honored by every staff who's worked here, and it's been passed down through the years without ever being broken. Even camp administration doesn't interfere." He cracked a grin. "Though they know they couldn't if they wanted to, eh? They'd have a revolt on their hands!"

A few staff did a quick jig, but grew quiet as Connor raised his hand.

"These are the rules," he said grandly. "There are very few, so even your basic minds should get it. Rule number one: During the day, obey the training manual at all times. Follow the orders of Erin Wood, our great and fearless leader."

His tone of contempt was obvious, and it was enhanced by further guffaws.

"Rule number two: After beddy-bye, when all the little kiddies are asleep in their beds, slip quietly into the woods to this midnight fire where the wild ones party." Cheers erupted. Connor waited for silence. "If you're on skills or maintenance, we'll expect you here every night. If you're a counselor, wait for the week you rotate onto maintenance or skills. If you've got campers who are *reeeeeally* sound sleepers, chance it. Rule number three: What goes on here is kept absolutely secret. There's nothing to be afraid of—just good times—but you will never speak of this place, not even among yourselves. Decade after decade, Camp Lakeshore staff have kept this pact. During the day, we are *so* pure. During the day, we act as if nothing is going on. But after beddy-bye, when the stars come out, the training manual is *trash*." Connor spat. "Here, Erin Wood has nothing to say and she knows it." His voice deepened. "Erin Wood," he said, then stomped his foot and grunted.

There were a few soft cheers. Connor raised a flashlight and played it over the faces of the new staff. "We have someone special with us tonight. A new recruit who happens to be the niece of our beloved leader, Erin Wood." Again, he did the stomp-grunt combo. "A sweet young thing by the name of Adrien." The flashlight found her face. "The Tuck'n Tack girl. Answer me, honey—are you the niece of Erin Wood?"

Adrien hesitated as several staff stomped and grunted. She might not be her aunt's biggest fan, but she knew Aunt Erin didn't deserve to have her head repeatedly stomped on by assholes, even as a metaphor. It was difficult to think with a flashlight square in her face and everyone watching, all of them older and well on their way to drunk.

Don't get smart, she thought to herself. *No one will protect you from your mouth.*

What for? she argued back savagely. *I could be dead tomorrow. I'm supposed to spend my last few hours kissing this guy's ass?*

"Yeah, Aunt Erin's in my family tree." Her voice wobbled, then came out clear. "So what?"

Connor's eyebrows lifted. "So you're going to be our special envoy, kiddo. You've got an in with the boss, and you're working in the office. When we need something, you'll get it for us. Gopher."

There were guffaws and cheers. Connor raised a pinkie and the noise subsided.

"No." Adrien's heart was pounding so hard, she thought The Big One was starting its final bright explosion. Then, suddenly, she was calm. The difficult part was over, the enormous choice had been made, and she knew who she was again: Grouch from the swamp. Social reject. The One Preparing For Death.

"This is shit." She turned from the line of new recruits and pushed through the others, who shifted to make room as she passed. At the edge of the group, she realized she wouldn't be able to find her way back in the dark. "I need a flashlight," she said, and to her surprise, she was handed one. She found the first white ribbon, then the next. Behind her, the revelry picked up as initiation rites continued. From a distance, it sounded like fun, and here she was, alone with her choice, stumbling through dark trees and cursing herself for shutting herself out. Why had she decided to work at Camp Lakeshore if she wasn't going to get along with anyone? Would it have been such a big deal to drink a beer and kiss someone's cowboy boot, or whatever stupid ritual they wanted her to perform?

But the stomp-grunt gesture still riled her. Why did they have to attack Aunt Erin behind her back? They acted like her biggest fans to her face. As she reached the cabin, Adrien shut off the flashlight, then turned and headed further through the woods to the clearing where the Wishing Tree stood. The moon had come out and the trunk was two beams of silvery light, one rising, one fallen. The leaves on both halves were still green. Surely it would live. More children than ever would leave their wishes here—every child knew what it meant to have a heart broken. Adrien placed both hands on the standing trunk and wished. Then she knelt and placed her hands on the fallen part and wished again—the same wish.

Something came back to her. Each time, she was washed by a cool green gentleness—both halves of the tree sent it into her, the standing and the fallen. So this part of Camp Lakeshore wasn't a scam. She wanted to weep, hug the tree and beg it to live for all the children who would come to it with open hands and broken hearts, looking for someone to bless and understand them.

"Geezzzus, Adrien, it's just a tree." She sat on the fallen half, head leaned against the standing trunk, feeling its strength. *Before and after*, she thought. They were still connected, weren't they? Still one and the same hope?

On her way to the cabin, she could see the spirits' dim glow on the lake. Even from a distance, she felt their writhing as if they were part of her—part of the way she breathed and knew things. It was the stamp of finality pulling her away from everyone normal, their good times. She just didn't belong in the land of the living.

Adrien turned and went alone into the empty cabin. When the other girls returned, she pretended to be dead. Darcie pretended right along with her.

five

The next morning, everyone acted as if nothing had happened.

"Morning, Grouch," Darcie said as Adrien opened her eyes.

"Morning, Spart," muttered Adrien, watching her roommate blow-dry her hair. Darcie had, of course, already showered. It looked like she would have her hair curled before Adrien managed to drag herself out of bed.

"So, what did you guys do after I left?" Adrien asked casually. Her roommate continued to dry her hair as if she hadn't spoken. Unsure if Darcie had heard the question, Adrien waited until the dryer went off, then said, "You guys talk about me after I left?"

Darcie angled the curling iron carefully over her left

eye and rolled up a strand of hair. "What d'you figure we'll be doing today, Grouch? More of the training manual, I bet. God, it's boring. I memorized the whole thing last year."

Adrien jerked angrily into a sitting position. "I asked you about last night. What happened after I left?"

"Left where?" Well-defined curls were springing up all over Darcie's head.

Fear beat a soft drum in Adrien's mouth. "Why're you doing this?" she whispered. "What did I ever do to you?"

For a second, Darcie froze. Then a bright, chipper look appeared on her face. "It's going to be a nice *day*," she said, stressing the last word. "I hope you have a great *day* to*day*, Grouch." She brushed out her curls, gave herself a satisfied glance in the mirror and pulled on a sweater. "Breakfast in five. Gotta go."

"Sure thing, Spart," Adrien muttered as her roommate went out the door. "Don't shoot any broken arrows."

"Hey, Mira!" Darcie sent her voice loudly down the hall. "Coming for breakfast?"

There was a sudden bout of whispering, then Darcie's cheerful, reproving voice. "It's going to be a nice *day*, don't you think, Mira? I hope I can get some practice in at the archery range."

"Oh yeah," said Mira loudly, catching on. "Oh yeah, it's a real nice *day*. I can see it's very sunny and bright out there."

The outer door slammed and Adrien sat up grouchily. So, it looked as if rule number three was going to be strictly obeyed ... by the obedient. If what Connor had said was true, she was the only disobedient staff in decades, which left no one else to disobey rule number three with, not even administration—not that she wanted to run to her aunt and tattle. Well, she could live with ignoring the whole thing as long as they left her alone. All they really wanted was her mouth shut so they could party. They sure weren't interested in her witty companionship or sparkling personality—probably the entire group was vastly relieved that the Doomsday Girl had rejected them.

The morning went by, absolutely normal. Everyone was friendly, just a little friendlier than yesterday. Even Connor made a point of saying good morning without evil undertones. He was in charge of the morning session by the beach, and began with a careful explanation of the waterfront safety regulations. The sunlight enhanced his hair dye, the wind ruffled his golden locks, and his biceps rippled. He was wearing his designer Camp Lakeshore T-shirt and he was gorgeous.

Adrien didn't see why she had to stand around listening to a hypocrite discuss the *rules* for sailboating, so early into Connor's spiel, she began edging into the trees, then turned and walked past the girls' cabins and the fenced-off septic pond. She veered left, avoiding the archery range, which was never to be approached from the south, and came out onto the road that led to the corrals. She had and hadn't been thinking about Paul, so when she caught sight of him working on another section of fencing, she was caught in a rush of confusion, wanting and not wanting the feelings that flew through her on raw wings. She was used to the guys at school, but not like this. Not with a slow wind riding the trees, not with the rich deep smell of earth so strong she could feel it in her skin. He wasn't even close and she felt like they were touching.

"Hey, Angel."

"I'm not Angel." Overdoing her anger made it easier to face him. He was smiling. So much happened in his face when he smiled. Whole stories told themselves.

"All right, *Adrien*. What're you doing up here?"

"Nothing. Much. Really." Words weren't doing the sentence thing. She stared intensely at the toe of his boot.

"So help me with this fence. Here, grab this." He handed her a rail and she held it as he hammered it into place.

"I'm supposed to be at Connor's sailboat session," she said, as if she owed Paul an explanation. "But ..."

"But what?" He straightened and looked at her. He was about an inch taller, his eyes were brownish-green, his lips a soft flush of red.

"Uh." She couldn't speak. "Last night ..."

"Initiation?" He turned back to the fence. "So, how'd it go?"

He was breaking rule number three! Finally, a partner in sanity. Her shyness vanished. "Did you have to do it?"

"They tried to make me last summer, but I'm never here at night. Wild man capers with city-slicker tough guys," he said softly. "What a blast."

She hesitated, unsure if he was including her. "They said Aunt Erin knows about it. I doubt it. She'd *never* let them get away with breaking all those rules."

"She knows," Paul said quietly. "She used to be summer staff. She went to deep-woods parties twenty years ago."

Adrien gaped. She could *not* imagine her aunt doing anything that ... social.

Paul grinned at her expression. "Who cares what they

do, as long as they don't tear down any buildings or raise the dead."

"But the training manual says—"

"They show up for their jobs in the morning and treat the kids okay. It's their business what they do in the middle of the night."

"Then why don't you go?" demanded Adrien.

"I don't like the company," he shrugged, then paused. "What exactly do they do out there, frolicking in the woods?"

"It's not *Lord of the Flies*," she said. "There aren't any sticks sharpened at both ends. It's mostly drinking. They make the new staff do something stupid, so I left."

"You don't like parties?"

"I didn't like the way they were talking about Aunt Erin," she burst out. "They suck up to her all day, then talk her down when they get out there at night. If they don't like her, they should act like it to her face."

"Like you do?"

"Yeah." She looked at him breathlessly, challenging him to tell her she was wrong. His eyes moved slowly over her face.

"You want a cigarette?" he asked. "I get a mid-morning break. C'mon, we'll go into the trees so no one sees us." He touched her bare arm and she almost cried out at the sudden heat.

"Um, here's fine," she said. "I, uh, like the horses."

His smile faded. "Sure. We'll watch the horses." He fished the pack out of his lumber jacket and handed her a cigarette. "Careful," he said, raising an eyebrow. "Smoking kills ten out of ten, y'know."

"D'you really believe," she asked slowly, "that you know exactly when and where you're going to die?"

He gave a short laugh and leaned on the fence, watching the horses at the other end of the paddock. After a pause, she realized that had been his response.

"Well, aren't you going to do something about it?" she demanded. "Make sure it doesn't happen?"

"What're you doing about yours?" he asked, not looking at her.

"I can't do anything, it's my brain. My blood vessels are warped. Yours aren't."

He stared moodily into the trees. "It's going to happen, one way or another."

"That's an attitude," she said flatly.

"Oh yeah?" He turned to look at her, his face derisive. "You're telling me I've been dreaming an *attitude* for two years? It's my *attitude* that keeps killing me a hundred different ways? You're telling me my *attitude* put you in my dreams before I ever saw or heard about you?"

He was so intense, the air about him throbbed. "No," she stammered. "That's not what I meant."

"Good," he said tersely. "I've got to get back to work."

He ducked through the rails and left her standing alone with her cigarette.

The girls in the photograph could have been from her classes at school. Swimsuits hadn't changed that much since the '70s, and neither had hairstyles. She wondered where they had come from, what they had returned to after their week at camp. Had Camp Lakeshore changed their lives, brought the shy ones out of their shells and taught the arrogant ones a lesson? Had they all made wishes at the Wishing Tree and had their wishes come true? They would be adults now, old enough to be her mother. How many of their children had experienced a brain aneurysm? Had any of them died?

It was Friday morning, the last day of Training Session. Adrien was alone in the cabin, sitting on her bed, skipping yet another staff activity. The only workshops she had attended all week had been led by Aunt Erin, Guy or Gwen, because they were the only instructors who would have noticed or cared about her absence. The lesson she was currently skipping dealt with wilderness camping, and was full of exciting scenarios such as where to set a tent on the side of a hill in a swarm of soldier ants with a storm brewing. After lunch, Connor would be leading a session on staff morale. Adrien had seen the list of exercises on Aunt Erin's desk. The first one involved standing on a fence post and falling backwards into the arms of fellow staff. Bonding was supposed to occur *if* they caught and cradled you. Fat chance she was showing up for that one.

Paul hadn't spoken to her since her killer comment about his attitude problem. Every time he saw her, a dark mood swallowed his face and he turned away. The guy could sure hold a grudge—her nic fits were driving her up a wall.

Darcie spoke to her only in passing. Adrien had woken several times in the middle of the night to see her roommate heading out or coming back in, but she didn't ask questions and Darcie didn't discuss anything. If staff looked suspiciously hungover in the morning, Aunt Erin didn't mention it. *Maybe she's used to it*, Adrien thought. *Maybe she always let them party hearty during Training Session*. Tomorrow, staff got the day off, and on Sunday the first wave of campers would arrive. Aunt Erin probably realized the night frolics would eventually fizzle out from sheer exhaustion.

Adrien was tired of trying to figure it all out. She was tired of everyone walking by with chipper smiles, tossing words at her that were supposed to matter. "Hey Grouch! How's it going, Grouch?" No one waited for an answer, they all hurried off to another workshop, the essential training manual tucked under an arm. Hypocrites. The whole place was a scam. If she reached out and actually touched someone, the person would probably dissolve into mist and fade away.

The only place she felt solid was standing by the lakeshore, watching the spirits. These past few days, their glow had been growing brighter. She had checked several times daily, and they were always there, floating on the water's surface. Watching them she felt at peace, drifting in a dream as vast as the lake, listening to the thousand tiny waves of her heart.

She leaned over the photograph, focusing on the five girls who clustered so close to Aunt Erin, they seemed like a single unit. They were the ones with the social telepathy, the girls who walked in a cabin door, scanned everyone and immediately recognized those who would become lifelong friends. Until her aneurysm, Adrien had fit right in. She had never thought about the stragglers, the outsiders. Now she looked at the three girls standing back from the group. Their smiles were wistful; they weren't so sure they were happy. Each carried a visible strike against her—two were chubby, one had braces, another wore glasses. In contrast, the girls at the center of the photograph looked as if they rode a constant ongoing laugh—if they glanced at each other the giggles would burst free, creating a separate universe to which only they belonged.

The girl under Aunt Erin's left arm was probably the leader. She had black shoulder-length hair and her nose was slightly beaked, but she was still pretty and she knew it. Her mouth was wide open; she looked loud, friendly and entirely oblivious to the existence of the three wistful girls in the background. She looked like every best friend Adrien had made during her Camp Lakeshore summers.

The cabin was suddenly cold. A slight wind had picked up, something different coming through the trees. In one corner of the room, a faint blur shifted, and a shiver ran down the back of Adrien's neck. Her breath stilled. She raised her eyes slowly, but the room rested empty of anything but the whispering green light. Whatever had just come from between the worlds to watch her was gone, but she knew it had been there. When she breathed again she breathed deeper, as if the air also came from a place beyond this one and she was breathing it in, pulling other worlds closer, until finally she would be able to see them and understand.

Adrien leaned against the fence at the archery range, watching her roommate. Darcie's hair was perfectly curled and her neon blue makeup glowed, but she wore a whistle around her neck and was speaking with *the voice of authority*. "No one," Darcie said emphatically, "absolutely no one is to step across this shooting line for any reason until I blow the whistle. If you notch your arrow improperly and it falls to the ground in front of you instead of flying through the air, too bad. Sometimes arrows from other people's bows fly sideways, and you can get hit just leaning over the line. If you're the stupid sucker who wastes a shot, leave it on the ground. If I catch you crossing that line, even *leaning* over it before I blow my whistle, you'll lose shooting privileges, got it?"

It was mid-afternoon. Connor had finished his morale booster, and staff had gathered for the last workshop of Training Session. It was the only one Adrien had been interested in attending. She hid a grin as Darcie glared ferociously at the group, trying to imprint on them the seriousness of the situation. "Grade five and six girls are *the worst*," she said with disgust. "They get the giggles and forget they've got a loaded bow. Someone makes a joke and they turn around to hear it." Darcie illustrated, whirling suddenly and pointing a loaded bow at the startled crowd. "If you've got a cabin of gigglers, you're going to have to give them a serious talk before they get here. I don't tolerate gigglers on my range. Understood?"

When enough staff had nodded, Darcie stopped pointing her loaded bow at them and moved into the proper stance for loading and shooting. Targets had been pinned to four straw bales at the opposite end of the range. They looked a long ways off. Adrien watched in disbelief as her roommate's first arrow sailed through the air and buried itself in a bull's eye. The group's mild clapping grew louder as Darcie repeated this act with her second and third arrows. "It's a short range," she said dismissively. "It's not hard to hit the target unless it's windy. It's for kids, after all."

Everyone joined one of the lines facing the targets, and Darcie handed the first person in each line three arrows. Adrien stood at the back and watched as arrows began wobbling, wiggling and whizzing through the air. Cheers and whistles accompanied the odd bull's eye, but no one managed consecutive ones, even Connor, who went first and hit the target every time. Once all twelve arrows had been released, Darcie blew her whistle, and the archers retrieved their arrows and handed them to the next person in line. Then Darcie wailed on her whistle and another round of shooting began.

Adrien managed to land her first arrow on the target's outer ring. Her next shot arced high and nose-dived, embedding itself in the ground. Her third flew over the back fence into the trees. "Way to go, Grouch," called the staff in her line, and turned back to their private conversations. Surrounded and alone, Adrien waited for Darcie's manic whistle, then headed onto the range with the other archers. Her first two arrows were easy to find, but the third would be difficult—the feathers that identified her set of arrows were green. Adrien went through the gate at the back of the range and pushed into the green shrubbery. Had her dumb green arrow gone high or low when it zoomed over the fence? Had it disappeared into this green bunch of leaves or that green bunch? She could hear staff pulling their arrows out of the targets and making jokes about being reincarnated as Robin Hood. "Get this," proclaimed one guy. "Robin Hood gets reincarnated as *me*." Boos and hisses accompanied this comment. Adrien pushed further into the greenery. Darcie had been adamant about returning with all three arrows. They were expensive to replace, and it taught *responsibility*. Grumpily, Adrien pushed through mosquitoes and poison ivy until her responsible foot knocked against the missing arrow. With her incredible skill and accuracy, she had managed to hit the ground twice. As she bent down to pull it out, she saw a yellow arrow embedded nearby. Feeling doubly responsible, she pulled them both out, then returned to the exit door at the south end of the range and pushed it open.

Arrows were coming straight at her. With a scream, Adrien ducked behind the nearest straw bale. An arrow thudded into the other side, and she jerked back. Her heart thudded, the whole world squeezed in and out of darkness; she could hear whimpering sounds and a far-off whistle. Then the air grew oddly quiet. There was the sound of running footsteps, and Darcie stepped behind the bale.

"You all right?" She was breathing heavily. "Grouch, did you get hit?"

Adrien crouched close to the ground, arms tight around herself. She couldn't stop shaking, even when Darcie knelt and hugged her. Everyone had been shooting at her. *Everyone* had been shooting *at her*.

"Some safety procedures," she hissed.

"It was an accident," said Darcie. "You took so long, I forgot you were out there."

"My group didn't have their arrows. They knew I was

out there. Why didn't they say something?"

Darcie's perfume was suffocating. Adrien wanted to pull away but couldn't. Not yet.

"I don't know," Darcie said uncomfortably, "but I'm the one in charge. I'm the one who let them shoot. It was an accident. I'm sorry, Grouch. I really am."

Darcie's apology was absolute and so was her hug. Safe and warm inside that hug, Adrien still couldn't stop thinking about Connor. While she was out looking for her lost arrow, he had rotated to the front of his line for a second round. In that split second before Adrien had realized there were three loaded bows pointed in her direction, she had gotten a clear glimpse of his smirk. He had just caught sight of her coming through the south exit door, and was shifting his bow from a target to her face.

It took Aunt Erin two seconds to notice the scrape on her niece's upper arm. "You get that at the range?" she asked immediately.

Adrien picked up the till to carry it out to Tuck'n Tack for staff candy hour. "Get what?"

She refused to think about the range. Huge hollow caves still echoed in her knees and gut. Aunt Erin came over and ran her finger over the scrape.

"Ow!" Adrien hissed.

"Arrow burn," said her aunt. "How'd this happen?"

"It didn't," said Adrien. "All right?"

Aunt Erin's voice was loaded. "You put down that till and talk."

Suddenly, holding onto the till took on overwhelming significance. Adrien stared rigidly out the screen door. Clouds were building over the lake. "I bumped into a tree branch while I was looking for an arrow. I didn't even notice my arm until you poked it."

She kept seeing Connor's smirk. If she told, Darcie was the one who would get into trouble, not him. It hadn't been Darcie's fault. Darcie had hugged her in front of the rest of the staff. She had hugged and hugged Adrien, helped her to her feet and walked with an arm around her, keeping her so close Adrien could feel her heart beat.

Had Connor's arrow been the one to graze her arm? Had it?

"I've got the rest of the afternoon," said Aunt Erin, folding her arms and parking her butt on the edge of her desk. "And so do you."

Adrien held onto the till and watched the bare wood floor. The wind grew louder, everywhere in the trees. Aunt Erin switched on the PA. "Darcie Smythe to the office. Darcie Smythe."

They waited in silence. *I could call Mom and Dad*, Adrien thought. *I could just go home.* But she could feel the clouds building on the lake like a promise. The sound of the wind moved through her as if she was part of its message, leaves lifting and falling inside her, whispering their meanings. The shaky hollow feeling faded and she felt part of this place, older than anything that could happen to her here, just like the trees, the lake and the sky were older than the camp. People were small stories that the wind blew clean, and then they were forgotten. One day, her story would be blown across the lake and she would be forgotten too. This didn't frighten her.

A shadow shifted through a patch of light on the floor, a writhing shape that lifted its arms to her, then faded. Adrien glanced at her aunt, but she was staring grimly at the door and hadn't seen the spirit. She also hadn't noticed that the clock above her desk had stopped at 1:37. Adrien glanced at the clock on the opposite wall. 3:55.

"Your clock stopped," said Adrien.

Aunt Erin glanced at it and lost the tight grip she kept on her face. For a moment, Adrien was staring at a face of absolute fear. Then her aunt's face closed over again. "Acting up, is it?" she muttered, moving toward it as Darcie's slow footsteps began to mount the outside steps. A slumped figure appeared in the doorway.

"Come in." Aunt Erin's voice was even, her pale eyes icy. Darcie took one step through the doorway and waited.

"Explain the arrow burn on my niece's arm," said Aunt Erin.

"It's not—" began Adrien.

"Yes, it is," Darcie said miserably.

"Adrien kept her mouth shut. Didn't betray you," said Aunt Erin. "Not her fault I'm firing you."

"What?" gasped Adrien.

Darcie blinked hard and stared at the dead clock. Then she nodded and turned to go. "Don't you even want to hear what happened?" demanded Adrien.

"Want a full explanation," said Aunt Erin, "but Darcie's fired just the same."

Facing the door, Darcie explained. Then she walked

out. The screen door slammed behind her.

"Open Tuck'n Tack," said Aunt Erin, fixing the clock.

"No," said Adrien. "I quit. I'm going home."

"Suit yourself," said Aunt Erin.

"I'm not *suiting myself*," hissed Adrien. "I *hate* you. You never give anyone a second chance. Darcie would *never* let it happen again."

"Could've been killed," said Aunt Erin, her eyes bright. "Don't get second chances when someone's dead."

"I'm not dead!" yelled Adrien. "No stupid arrow's going to kill me—you know that. I'll die the way I'm going to die, and nothing's going to stop it. You could fire a million staff and nothing would stop it."

"Got nothing to do with it," snapped Aunt Erin. "Her carelessness almost got someone killed."

"None of them can shoot," howled Adrien. "Only Darcie can aim and she wasn't shooting."

"Got your arm."

"Lucky chance." Adrien stomped the floor. "You make me so *mad*. Give her a break. That stupid archery range'll be safer than a daycare after this."

Aunt Erin sat quietly on the edge of the desk. Abruptly, Adrien realized how closely she was being watched.

"You like rooming with Darcie?" Aunt Erin asked.

"She's all right," Adrien said grudgingly. "I never knew Robin Hood wore nail polish."

Aunt Erin cracked a slow smile and rocked once. Head back, she took a deep breath and her face relaxed. "Maybe I was too hasty," she said. "You find Darcie and tell her to come talk to me."

"You won't fire her?"

"We'll work things out." Aunt Erin's eyes had taken on a whole different shade of pale blue. The ice was melting.

"THANKS!" Adrien dumped the till and raced to the door.

"Oh, and Adrien," called Aunt Erin.

"What?" asked Adrien, turning back.

"You give life a second chance too," said Aunt Erin.

six

Adrien wandered through the wooded area surrounding the cabins set aside for the older girls. She wanted to go down by the lake, but she could see Connor and a few others ignoring the cloud cover and getting into canoes for a paddle before supper. She was supposed to be working in Tuck'n Tack, but she couldn't get at the key or the till because Darcie was in the office talking to Aunt Erin. A DO NOT DISTURB sign had been posted on the door.

The mayflies were definitely dying off. It was the last Friday in June and the ground was littered with their brown withered bodies. She pulled seven live ones off her shirt and watched them flutter away. At the start of Training Session, it would have been twenty-five. In just over a week, they would all be gone.

Voices and laughter were coming from the cabin that was called Prairie Sky. Adrien stopped. These cabins were supposed to be empty until Sunday when the campers arrived, but as she listened, another peal of laughter floated out of a window. Prairie Sky was closest to the lake, the only cabin in this section that she had never stayed in. Still, she knew what it would look like. Each cabin held five bunk beds and several dressers. She had always grabbed a top bunk and spent her week sleeping mid-air, drifting on the ebb and flow of the other girls' breathing.

The windows were open, airing the place out. Standing on tiptoe, she could just see in. At first there was nothing, just the quiet green light filtering through the trees. Then she glimpsed something in a corner—someone turning, part of her visible, but transparent. It was the girl from the photograph, the one with the beaked nose and the wide laughing mouth. She was laughing now, her voice clear, and then she spoke.

"What would Erin do if she knew we were spying on the guys' cabins?"

"She'd probably want to come along." A second girl came into view, also transparent but recognizable with her long red ponytail, tube top and shorts—another of the five girls grouped close to Aunt Erin. "Especially if we picked Spruce Hollow. Sure wish we had Peter Pecker for our counselor. Think he could wear tighter swim trunks?"

"Not and still get into them." This voice belonged to a girl sitting on a top bunk. All Adrien could see of her were vague swinging legs.

"*You think Erin will get into them?*" asked the first girl.

There was another peal of laughter.

"*She's sure been watching him,*" said a fourth voice, out of Adrien's line of sight. "*I was almost drowning at swim class yesterday, and she didn't even notice.*"

"*We should set them up.*" Arms outstretched, the first girl spun a thoughtful pirouette. "*Then spy on them. I'd give them twenty minutes to complete the dirty deed.*"

"*You only need three.*" Another girl walked into view. The last of the photograph's laughing group of five, she had short blond-brown hair with obvious highlights, and was pulling on a swimsuit, careless of who watched.

"*You only need three, Nat,*" said the first girl, stopping her pirouette. "*Most people do more than grunt and jump each other, you know. Erin would want time to … ease into it.*"

Giggles erupted. The girl with the swinging legs fell backwards, kicking her legs with glee.

"*How would you know?*" asked Nat, now fully dressed and fluffing her hair. "*I'm the only one here who's done it.*"

"*Yeah, you did it,*" said the first girl. "*But did you enjoy it? That's what I'd like to know.*"

Nat ignored her.

The legs resumed their swinging. "*D'you think he'd kiss her first, or would she kiss him?*"

"*He'd kiss her.*" Nat's reply was automatic.

"*D'you think he'd touch her boobs?*" asked the legs.

"*If they were going to get anywhere.*"

Adrien was getting hot and bothered. She hadn't had girlfriends since she was thirteen, when French kissing had been the hot topic. There had been jokes about groping, but no one had *gotten this graphic about what came after.*

"D'you think she'd touch his—"

The voices and outlines of the girls vanished, and Adrien whimpered in disappointment. Just when it had been getting interesting. They had been talking about *Aunt Erin*.

"Watching the dead?"

Adrien whirled. Paul stood in the clearing at the front of the cabin, holding a dark brown bottle. She sagged against the cabin wall.

"Don't sneak up on me like that."

"Sorry. That cabin's haunted. See any ghosts?"

"No," she said immediately. "I stayed in this cabin once. Nostalgia, you know."

"Door's open," said Paul. "Just walk in and get fully nostalgic."

"In a haunted cabin? No thanks." She wasn't sure why she was lying. For the past three years, everything in her life had been private, separate. She had grown used to holding experiences to herself, the way she had clutched the till in Aunt Erin's office. Who would she be if she let go?

"The nurse is off until Sunday, so Erin sent me to doctor you." He produced a package of cotton batting and unscrewed the bottle cap.

"It's just a scrape," Adrien said, stepping back.

Paul shrugged. "Erin's hyper about this kind of stuff. Lose a hangnail, she'll send you to Emerg. C'mon, I just have to clean it, make sure you aren't about to croak."

"What makes you an expert?"

He made a few harsh croaking noises. "On the verge."

Adrien grinned reluctantly, then slowly extended her

arm. The whole thing felt awkward, the air stiff and uncomfortable, full of echoes: *It's going to happen, one way or another. That's an attitude. It's my attitude that keeps killing me a hundred different ways?*

"How'd you know where I was?" She winced as the hydrogen peroxide settled into the broken skin.

"Sniffed you out." He leaned close, wiping away a trickle of dry blood. "I can do that sometimes."

"Creepy," said Adrien. "Aunt Erin says you have a sixth sense."

"Maybe." He swabbed the sore area, examining every stinging millimeter. She wanted to pull away from the pain, but his dark hair was tickling her cheek, and her brain was going soft and fuzzy. She wanted to smell his hair, she wanted to brush her lips across it, she wanted ... He looked up, his eyes on her slightly open mouth.

"Whose arrow was it?" he asked.

"I don't know."

"Take a guess."

"A lot of people were shooting."

"Adrien, you get shot by an arrow *and* you're seeing ghosts. Something's going on here."

Her chin went up and she stepped back. "You don't talk to me for days, and now you think you can just tell me what's going on in my life? I told you, I didn't see any ghosts. And the arrow was an accident."

"I doubt it." He stepped forward; she took another step back. "There's a strange light around you," he said quietly. "You glow. Like you're standing in the light from some other place."

She opened her mouth, then closed it. The silence

around them was tremendous.

"That first day," said Paul, "down by the lake, I saw past you. You were sitting in the lifeguard's chair and just beyond you, in the sky, was a huge opening. There was another world there, full of others. Others who've passed through. They were watching you."

Adrien's head was full of tiny falling things. She turned from his dark staring eyes and ran into the whisper of the knowing trees.

She woke suddenly to someone leaning over her in the dark. From the perfume she knew it was Darcie, but still Adrien feigned sleep, listening to the other girl's soft uneven breathing. It was the middle of the night; Darcie was either heading out to the campfire or coming back in. What could she possibly want now—to drag Adrien with her a second time? To deliver a nasty message from Connor? After her conversation in the office with Aunt Erin, Darcie had spent the evening campfire watching Adrien, her face twisted in thought that was obviously new territory, but the two girls hadn't spoken since Adrien had run into the cabin that afternoon and pulled Darcie's duffel bag out of her hands, panting so hard she could barely get the words out: "You're not fired. Aunt Erin says she made a mistake. Go talk to her. Now." When Darcie had hesitated, a proud grimace on her face, Adrien had burst out with a raw "Please!"

Why had it mattered so much? For that second while Darcie wavered, Adrien had thought her heart would split wide open with panic, but finally Darcie had turned, tight-lipped, and left the cabin. Adrien had sunk down onto the bed, next to the pile of makeup and clothing her roommate had been about to shove into the stinky duffel bag, and the next few minutes had been complete exhaustion. When the air had begun to move again, she had put everything away where it belonged—the perfume and nail polish on the dresser, the duffel bag under the bed, the frilly lacy underwear in the dresser drawers.

Now, in the dark, Darcie's hand brushed her shoulder. Adrien kept her eyes closed.

"You surprised me, Grouch." Darcie's voice whispered within itself, so quiet it was almost thought. "Your aunt told me what you said. I never would've thought you'd stick up for me. I thought you hated all of us, maybe me the most, but I guess you don't. I guess you really think the campfire's stupid. Well, I'm going to tell you something. I think it's stupid too, but I don't have your guts. Or maybe I like people more, I don't know. But from now on, I'm your friend. I'll stick up for you, I promise." There was a quiet pause, filled with Darcie's soft puffy breathing. Then she straightened and moved to the door. "One last thing, Grouch. I know you're awake. I know you heard what I just said. When I promise something, I mean it. We're friends, whatever that takes."

Without waiting for an answer, Darcie slipped out the door. Adrien listened to the sounds of the other girls following her. Then they were gone, fading into the night, heading off to do whatever it was they did around the campfire when Aunt Erin wasn't watching. She lay a while longer, then sat up. The night air felt full of huge places, shifting and rearranging. That afternoon, talking to Paul, she had been afraid, but now she was restless, stirred by dark currents and far from sleep. Slipping on a pair of jeans and her father's lumber jacket, she left the cabin and headed through the woods toward the lake, then cut across the lawn to the older girls' cabins, just inside the trees.

Prairie Sky loomed dark and silent, no transparent girls giggling in their beds. Had they actually been *ghosts* like Paul said, or had she imagined them because she had stared so long at the photograph? And why had there only been five? Where were the other three girls Aunt Erin had counseled that week?

She saw them as she came through the trees onto the ridge above the beach, their gray smoky glow floating on the water's surface—the spirits of five girls splayed as if in sleep. She felt the certainty of it then, like cold water swamping her face. The girls she had seen that afternoon in Prairie Sky were the five girls in her aunt's photograph, and they had all died somehow, while they were young. For some reason their spirits had returned to haunt the lake. But why? Were their deaths the reason her aunt prowled the campground in the dark, the reason Adrien had caught her on the beach that first night, staring out at the water? Something connected Aunt Erin to those spirits, and it was more than the fact that she had been their counselor while they were alive. Why else would she keep a photograph of them under the mat on her desk, where she could slip it out and look at it several times a day? *Don't get second chances when someone's dead*. Some deep tragedy had hold of her, a mystery that linked her to the five girls' deaths, something no one ever talked about, including Adrien's parents. If any staff at Camp Lakeshore knew, they were keeping quiet out of respect for Aunt Erin. The secret had been completely buried, just like the girls' bodies must have been.

But the girls weren't keeping themselves buried. Adrien had seen them again at supper, lined up in front of the dining hall, their five faces pretending to be quiet and well-behaved so they could get in for food. There had been just a glimpse of them, and then they had disappeared. Staff had walked through the place the girls had been standing without a flicker of awareness, and when Adrien had stepped into it there had been nothing, not even the whisper of a girl's voice, her far-off laughter.

She sat on the ridge and watched the spirits. They seemed to be sleeping, drifting on invisible currents but always together, as if they were a single unit. That afternoon, she had heard their voices and learned one of their names—Nat. Short for Natalie? What were the rest of their names? What were their stories? And why were the girls appearing to her both before *and* after, alive *and* dead? They seemed trapped between worlds, unsure where they belonged, just like she was.

The lake lapped at the shore, quiet but uneasy. The ground was covered with dead wings. Adrien realized she was probably staining the seat of her jeans and was about to get up when someone sat down beside her, bumping her knee. Turning, she saw Connor, his hair phosphorescent in the moonlight. A coldness crept through her, and she went very still. A ways down the beach, a frog called slow and steady. The moon shone lonely and empty, the silent campground stretched behind them. The rest of the staff would be at the campfire now, but Aunt Erin, Guy and Gwen were nearby, sleeping in their beds like normal people. If she needed to, she would scream. She would pull the dead out of the ground with her screaming.

"So this is where you hang out at night." Connor scanned the water, his voice conversational. She wondered if he could see the spirits, if the spirits could see the two humans sitting on the night edge of the lake. If she spoke, maybe she would feel less fear.

"Why aren't you doing your campfire thing?"

He was several inches taller, and so close she could smell his shampoo. He plucked a stalk of grass and began shredding it. "Just looking for my lost arrows," he said softly.

"Yeah, well, I found mine." She started to get up, but he grabbed her wrist.

"C'mon." His face was suddenly full of smiles. "I saw you sitting here, so I came over to check out your arm. How's your arm, Adrien?"

"It'd be fine," she said, "if you let go of it."

He started rubbing her shoulder. "Let's make pax, eh? I don't want to spend my summer fighting with the boss's niece. Erin'll fire me if you don't like me."

"Stop touching me."

"Pax?" He slid an arm around her, and she pushed at him.

"Pax or kiss my ass?" she hissed.

He let go of her then. "Either."

The lake lapped at their ears; the beach was a calm splash of moonlight. For an odd moment, his eyes lingered on her mouth. Her heart pounded.

"Neither," she said harshly.

He jumped off the ridge, taking the steep drop to the sand and landing on his feet. "This is neither. I'll take you midnight canoeing."

"Isn't that against the rules?"

"They're my rules. I'm in charge of waterfront. I won't tell, you won't tell. It'll be our secret."

She hesitated, and he stepped closer. "Listen." His voice was suddenly hoarse, his face almost frightened. "It was a joke, okay? I didn't mean to hit you with that arrow, I swear."

"Well, you did."

"I'm sorry," he said. "Look, I apologize. It was a dumb, stupid, dork-brain thing to do."

He stood in front of her, one hand outstretched—tall, broad-shouldered, probably twenty-one. It was a moment to take hold of, a moment that could change things. Any one of the five girls from Prairie Sky would have jumped at the chance. Adrien wavered. Maybe she was overreacting. Like he said, it was nothing more than a joke gone wrong. She hadn't *died*, after all. Everyone made mistakes, didn't they? Here was an opportunity to make pax, go night canoeing and come back different, laughing and carefree like a popular girl. She would be popular if Connor liked her, she would have friends …

Out on the water the spirits were rising, their arms reaching toward her, their mouths opening in a low wail. Their sound twisted through her; every fiber in her body vibrated with the long thin moans of the dead girls on the lake.

"Maybe not tonight," she said uncertainly, watching

them. "I'm tired."

"You're not scared of a little water, are you?" He stepped closer, looking up at her. "Is it your aunt you're worried about? I can handle her."

She remembered the stomp-grunt combo. Her head cleared and she couldn't believe she had been about to get in a canoe with this jerk. "You're lucky she doesn't know about your campfire shit."

"Oh, she knows," he said. "The sweet boss knows, all right."

In spite of what Paul had told her, Adrien couldn't believe her aunt would *ever* have snuck out to any middle-of-the-night campfires, even twenty years ago. She gave a scornful laugh. "She'd fire you so fast."

Connor raised his hands, still smiling. "It's a tradition. Hey, it's been around longer than she has. Goes back as long as Camp Lakeshore." He took a step forward. "What d'you think your precious auntie did at night when she first started working here?"

"Not that." Wild fury rose in her. "She was a *counselor*, not skills or maintenance. She had kids to take care of, she would've been responsible."

Connor started to laugh.

"Stop laughing," she demanded. "And stop talking about her like that."

He passed a hand over his face, wiping the laughter clean. For a moment he stood motionless and gorgeous in the moonlight, then took a sudden run up the path and jogged across the lawn toward the trees. "Beer calls," he waved. "Ta-ta …"

She turned back to the spirits. They had stopped wailing and were floating on the quiet water, their bodies intertwined as if they were extensions of one another. She wasn't certain, but she thought they were watching her. Closer than a mother, closer than a father. Closer than any aunt. The spirits watched her the way she watched them.

"I love you," she whispered to the five dead girls. Then she turned, heading across the lawn to her empty cabin, the loneliness that would not leave her, the deep dreaming sleep.

seven

Saturday morning, Adrien sat on the office steps and watched joking groups of staff climb into cars and drive away. Dressed in shorts and swimsuits, they carried hats and sunscreen, and were headed for a nearby public beach. Usually, she received at least a few calls of "Hey Grouch, how's the swamp?" but today no one waved or spoke to her. After last night's chat on the beach, Connor must have told everyone at the campfire to give her the cold shoulder for refusing pax. She felt invisible, part of another dimension. When she saw Darcie approaching, arm-in-arm with Connor, laughing and bumping hips, Adrien retreated into the office and watched from a window as they climbed into Connor's Toyota. Several others joined them, but her stomach still felt like the bottom of a lake. So much for her roommate's promise of eternal friendship.

Spitting gravel, the Toyota drove off. Adrien returned to the porch steps. As the last cars left, a rustling quiet descended on the grounds. Birds called back and forth. Far off, the lake glinted. She plucked off a few mayflies and picked at a mosquito bite. A faint buzz could be heard coming down the road, a single vehicle traveling into the grounds—someone who had forgotten sunscreen?

She thought about staking out Prairie Sky, spying on the girls who had stayed there twenty years ago. But was it spying? She hadn't gone looking for them, and she hadn't asked to see their spirits. It was almost as if they were showing themselves to her. Sometime during the night, she had woken to find herself sleeping in a cabin full of girls her own age. She had been lying in an upper bunk, and the sounds of the other girls' deep sleep-breathing had risen toward her, rocking her like a cradle. *Not alone, not alone.* For a brief moment, she and the girls had dreamed together—something about water, endless gentle water. Then she had woken a second time to see Darcie's empty bed. The only sounds in the cabin had been her own.

A dirt bike pulled onto the walkway in front of her and stopped. A helmet hid the rider's face, but she recognized his butt. Paul cut the engine. "Want a ride?"

Adrien was caught in the sudden wild beating of her heart. "A ride where?"

He unstrapped a second helmet from the handlebars and handed it to her. "You ever been dirt biking?"

"No." She stared at the helmet in her hands. She had thought this day would belong to the usual loneliness, but it was changing shape, new places opening in the air, in her mind. She put the helmet on slowly.

"Leave a note for Erin," said Paul.

"Why?"

"You're her niece. It's genetic—she'll worry."

Adrien had never even *thought* about being on a dirt bike. Her mother got antsy if she looked at a twelve-speed. Cautiously, she got on behind Paul. She tried to leave some room, but the angle of the seat slid her up against his butt. They were plastered together.

"Use the foot rests," Paul hollered as the engine roared to life. "And hang on. I'm your seatbelt."

She hesitated. This was starting to feel like a massage parlor. Then he gunned the bike, it jumped forward, and she had to grab something to stay on. By the time her head cleared, they were passing the corrals, and her arms were wrapped around him in a death grip. How embarrassing. But this was nothing like being in a car—the ground went by at an alarming speed, and it looked so close. Instinctively, her arms tightened. Paul stopped at the edge of the grounds, where the camp road connected to a highway. A few cars whizzed by.

"You all right?" he asked.

"Yeah," she said to his helmet.

"Don't let go," he said, and turned onto a well-worn dirt path that ran parallel to the highway. The track dipped and swerved through blond grass that rose to her waist and brushed her bare arms. There was the constant thrum of the engine beneath her, the warm shift of Paul's back against her chest. Everything was sun, wind and sky. They came to a split in the trail and he took the path leading away from the highway, across a scrubby field and up a hill. When they crested, he stopped briefly. Ahead lay a series of hills, laced with dirt paths. Several bikes jetted puffs of dust as they skidded and swerved.

Paul turned his head. "Cousins."

Great, a family reunion. "You're not going to do that, are you?" she asked, pointing to a bike that was mid-air, coming off a ridge.

"You'll be okay if you keep hanging on like that," he grinned.

Flushing, she let go. Paul took her hands and pulled them back around his waist.

"Keep your seatbelt fastened." He revved the engine.

Adrien gave an exasperated snort, but lost the irritation. She couldn't stop breathing the warm grass scent, couldn't stop *knowing* she was breathing. Above spread a sheer blue sky. It felt like the dome of her brain, as if her skull had lifted off and she was one with an endless blue, floating above the rippling blond hills. "It's so pretty out here."

"Yeah," said Paul, "it is."

A shout came from below as the other bikers caught sight of them. Paul stuck two fingers into his mouth and gave an ear-splitting whistle. Ear-splitting whistles replied.

"Found your wings yet, Angel?" he asked.

"Adrien," she said automatically, still watching the sky.

"Well, Adrien." He leaned forward, pulling her with him. "Let's fly." With a spurt, the bike careened downward, leaving her scream at the crest of the hill. The next hour was a blurred weave of beige grass and brown earth, following paths that rose toward sky, then descended again. She soon felt it, a liquid ceaseless flight that could have been a fantasy of riding the wind, but for the sound of the engine and the feel of Paul's body pulling her into the swerve of the bike. After a while, she lost even this and became only motion, riding earth, cresting sky, catching the sun in her mouth and letting it out again into the endless blue. When Paul finally cut the engine, the silence was shattering. She pulled off her helmet, and her ears vibrated with the quiet. As she slid off the bike, every part of her body ached—her arms, the inside of her legs, even her butt. Gradually, sound returned and she could hear the wind sighing in the grass, the distant whine of the other bikes. Paul spoke, his voice so complete, it seemed to rise out of the earth.

"How'd you like it?" He stood beside her, running his hands through his sweaty hair. The usual heaviness that sat on him was gone, as if he had dumped his sixth sense for the day and was living inside the other five.

She breathed the deep warm scent of grass and earth. "I want my own bike," she said. "I want my own bunch of hills. And I want this sky."

He grinned. "You want a smoke?"

"Yeah, *and* lunch. *And* a bathroom."

He pointed to a large rock with a small shadow, the only privacy the area offered. As she squatted, her knees creaked and the ground still seemed to be moving, but desperation made do. When she returned, Paul was sitting on the ground, talking to one of his cousins. The other bikers were a crest of noise, cruising toward them.

"So, who's your girlfriend?" asked the skinny nervous-looking cousin, obviously known for his tact.

"Adrien," said Paul, handing her a pack of cigarettes. "She works at Camp Lakeshore. Adrien, this is Rene."

Rene had mastered the art of checking out a girl with his peripheral vision. He gave her a sideways grin. "So, you like biking?"

"Paul's giving me his bike," Adrien said immediately. "At the end of the day it's staying with me and he's walking home."

Paul gave a soft laugh.

"Engaged already." Rene gave Paul's shoulder a congratulatory pat. Adrien concentrated on lighting a cigarette as the other cousins pulled off their helmets and were introduced—Claude, Philippe and Bette, a burly short-haired red-head who could be taken for a boy at a glance. As they talked about an upcoming rodeo, Adrien sat stripping grass, watching from her usual position outside the conversation. Except this time the earth vibrated like the roar of a bike, and her blood was madly cruising every artery. Her stomach let loose with a loud grumble and she stood.

"I need food," she said to Paul.

"Yup, me too." He pulled on his helmet. "See you guys."

"Invite us to the wedding," Rene called as they got onto the bike. Adrien's body settled into its worst aches. Paul waved and they swung onto the track. Now that she had been called his girlfriend, holding onto him was different. When they touched, her skin felt warm and sweet. Why hadn't Paul told Rene they just shared smokes and talked?

"Where are we going?" she yelled at his helmet.

"Food," he yelled back. A short while later, they pulled up in front of a farmhouse. Paul cut the engine. In the sudden quiet, she tried but couldn't move. The slightest shift was torture.

"Stiff?" Paul slid awkwardly off the front of the seat and turned to help her.

"Rigor mortis," she groaned.

He gave a soft grin. His eyes were like moss, velvety. "Hold still." He undid her helmet and took it off. Then he reached into her hair and gently removed something. It was a mayfly, its pale wings slightly mangled, but alive. "Hitched a ride," said Paul. They watched it wobble off his hand, flutter a short distance and disappear into the grass.

"Won't last long."

"Who does?"

"I'm glad I lasted longer than two days."

"Two days is eighty years to them," said Paul. "Imagine what it'd be like if life was just water and grass and sky. Heaven, don't you think?"

"Earth," said Adrien. "What kind of life is it to live at the bottom of a lake for two years, so you can fly for two days, spawn and die?"

"I like the middle part," he said. "I bet they make every second count."

She had never felt so much heat. Concentrating furiously, she lugged her aching body off the bike, just as a small girl in overalls and braids came running up, an aging collie loping along behind her.

"Who's she?" demanded the girl.

"*She* is Adrien, Michelle," said Paul.

"Why is her face so red?"

The red deepened. Desperately, Adrien wished for The Big One.

"Windburn," said Paul. He touched her arm, and Adrien managed a sideways glance. "C'mon in for lunch."

They headed for the front porch, Michelle trailing behind. "She's your girlfriend," the little girl announced, "because Leanne dumped you, and now you don't got one."

Something shot through Adrien, hot and painful.

"Leanne moved to Regina," Paul said stiffly. "And we were just friends."

"I saw you kissing her," Michelle insisted shrilly.

Paul took a deep breath and glanced at Adrien. "How stiff are you? Need help climbing the stairs?"

She looked away. "I'll be all right."

"Hope you're hungry." He took the steps in a single bound. "We've got loads of food."

Food turned out to mean everything from baked beans to leftover lasagna to angel food cake, with a few sardines thrown in for dessert. Paul's mother hovered about the kitchen, wearing overalls and braids like her daughter, constant movement and chatter. She watched Adrien, and Adrien watched her.

"Now Michelle, you've already had your lunch, and you had two pieces of cake, and why are you wearing your shoes in the kitchen? Take this out to Sheltee, she's losing too much weight. Adrien, Paul tells me you're Erin Wood's niece. She's been a good solid camp director all these years, don't you think? This is the day I always think of it, all

those young ones packing their suitcases and sleeping bags
for their first week at camp. I remember when your city
cousin Annette used to go, Paul. Always wanted to take
half the house. Couldn't fit it all—"

The window curtains gusted sharply, and the air
changed. City air—Adrien could smell the difference. As
she watched, the Marchands' kitchen walls darkened to
burgundy-blue, Paul and his mother faded, and then a different room came into view—a bedroom that looked normal but felt too intense, like breathing in a dream. A girl
walked into this bedroom, set a suitcase on the bed and
opened it. It was one of the girls from the photograph, the
one who laughed the loudest, the one Adrien would have
chosen first as a friend. Pulling out a dresser drawer, she
started chucking underwear and socks into the suitcase as
if it was a basketball hoop.

*"Roberta," called a voice. A look-alike woman appeared in
the doorway, carrying a load of folded laundry. "Seven pairs of
socks and seven pairs of underwear," she admonished. "Last year
you took twice as many and lost most of them."*

*"The guys do panty raids, Mom," Roberta protested. "I need
extra, or I won't have any left."*

*"Seven of each," her mother said firmly. "Your jeans are in the
dryer." She went out again.*

*Roberta turned toward the suitcase, muttering, "How can I
help it if my gotch are popular?" Dramatically, she counted out
seven pairs of socks and underwear, and tossed the rest onto the
floor. Then she began to pack the laundry her mother had brought
in. She hummed to herself, an old tune about a bullfrog named
Jeremiah who liked to share wine.*

Something else drifted into the bedroom, a human shape twisting in a gray smoky haze—one of the five spirits from the lake. The girl continued to hum and pack, not noticing as the spirit tucked extra articles into the suitcase—a skull, a femur, part of a pelvis. Spirit bones, they shimmered with a gray glow, Roberta's hands passing directly through them as she folded, patted and counted. She and the spirit looked so comfortable together, the spirit weaving itself in a caress about the humming girl, as if it was nothing more than the lilt of her voice.

Then it turned, and Adrien felt the spirit look directly at her, as if it knew she was watching, as if it had brought this moment to her and laid it open in her mind like a gift.

She was back in the Marchands' kitchen. The radio was tuned to a golden oldies station, and Three Dog Night was singing "Joy to the World." Mrs. Marchand was still talking, Michelle calling to her from outside.

"What could that girl want now?" Mrs. Marchand sighed, going out the door.

"Adrien?" Paul leaned forward, watching her closely. "Where the hell are you?"

She stared at him, her eyes straining to return to the bedroom where a girl and her spirit packed life and death into the same suitcase.

"I—" stammered Adrien. "I just had a daydream, but it was so real. I saw a girl Aunt Erin counseled twenty years ago. She's one of the ghosts from Prairie Sky. She wasn't dead yet, she was getting ready to come to camp—packing, like your mom said camp kids would be doing today. In my daydream, the girl's spirit was beside her, out-side her body, like she was both dead and alive at the same time, and it was packing *bones* into her suitcase. She must've died while she was at *camp*. I bet you that's what it means. I bet you Aunt Erin had five campers who all died at Camp Lakeshore while she was their counselor. That's why Prairie Sky is haunted. That's why their spirits are on the lake."

Paul let out a slow whoosh of air. "So you *did* see ghosts in Prairie Sky."

"I've been seeing them all over the camp," Adrien muttered. "Almost from the minute I got there. Don't you see them?"

He shook his head. "I just feel something. The dead don't talk to me."

"They're not talking to me, just … showing me things. Their lives." Her eyes hung onto his face. "I feel like they've got something to tell me."

"But they're *dead*," he said intensely. "Why would the dead want to talk to you?"

"They don't feel dead," she said. "They feel … like me."

"They don't creep you out?"

"Do I creep you out?"

"You're not dead."

"Yet," she said.

He went still as caught breath, and she watched thoughts pass through his face. Finally he nodded, as if they had come to an agreement and the understanding between them was complete.

"*Yet*," he said softly. "That's what we've got—you and me."

That afternoon they rode for hours, just the two of them, past fields of wheat and canola, farmhouses and barking dogs—a world they passed through, but were no longer part of. They knew now, accepted, that they had been set aside, chosen for a mystery that was fast approaching. They could ignore it, try to hide from it or ride toward it in a thin grim line, seeking its face. All afternoon, they rode seeking. After a while, they removed their helmets. Paul strapped them to the bike and they rode full into the wind, Adrien resting her face on his back while her hair flew free. She no longer thought about holding onto him—they had become part of sun, sky and wind. For hours that afternoon, they did not touch ground. They lifted above the sound of the bike and flew in their wild seeking heartbeats, until it was time to return to earth again.

When Paul turned onto the Camp Lakeshore road, Adrien came back to herself, the stiff ache of her body, the warm sweat of his back. *Paul's back—she was all over him.* She tried to straighten, but the ache in her muscles let loose with pure fire. When he stopped a short way up the road, out of sight of the office, she dragged herself off and stood holding her back in disbelief.

"It'll wear off." Paul's voice cracked after its afternoon of silence.

"How long am I going to feel like this?" she groaned.

Before she could move, he was holding her. All the warmth in the world stepped close and wrapped its arms around her, Paul's face in her tangled hair, his breathing in her neck. A wild longing came through her; she saw herself doing things she had never imagined. Slowly, she put her arms around him, let herself touch his sweaty back. He was trembling.

"Sometimes it's fire," he said softly. "I can smell my skin burning. Or it's drowning, and I'm begging for air. Lots of times, it's falling. I'm caught in an endless fall, and I never know when I'm gonna crash."

"What day is it?" she asked hoarsely. "What day are you supposed to die?"

"My birthday." His arms tightened and a gust of sound came out of him. "God, I want to live."

Pulling free, he turned quickly, mounted his bike and rode off. She stood in the scent and whisper of trees, watching him go, and saw the late-afternoon sun touch long golden fingers to what looked like the beginning of wings on his back, fragile and iridescent as a mayfly's.

Adrien found her aunt in Prairie Sky, sitting on one of the bottom bunks. She stepped through the doorway and looked around, trying to see it for the first time as Roberta would have. Who would she be looking at? Nat? The girl with the red ponytail?

The cabin wavered slightly and someone took shape, turning toward Adrien—a young woman with a tall proud face, blond straight-falling hair, the palest blue eyes. Twenty years ago, Erin Wood had carried the world like a scenic backdrop. Anyone seeing her for the first time would have been mesmerized—Roberta, that entire cabin of girls. Adrien blinked, the young Erin Wood vanished, and her thirty-eight-year-old aunt came into view, lines drawn deeply about the mouth and eyes, but the shoulders holding firm.

"Aunt Erin." Adrien walked slowly toward her aunt, the evening deepening about her, secret worlds watching from the other side of consciousness. "I want to give this back." The photograph fluttered between her fingers, a moment from the past that held so many meanings. As her aunt caught sight of it, her shoulders slumped and her mouth sucked in. She took it gently, careful not to touch the center and stain what was left of that twenty-year-old laughter.

"I found it in the office," Adrien said. "I'm sorry I didn't give it to you when you asked."

"Why didn't you?" asked her aunt, staring at the past.

"There was something I didn't understand then."

"And what is that?"

"You called me here." Adrien pointed to the photograph. "And so did those girls."

Their eyes caught, Aunt Erin's mouth coming open in a question she couldn't ask. A surge of strength came through Adrien—she felt strong and solid. At the same time, she was hazy and insubstantial as smoke, The Big One hidden and waiting in the core of her brain.

"Whatever happens," Adrien said slowly, "this summer is mine."

She took a deep breath, tasting the scent of spruce. Then she turned and stepped through the doorway, out into the late green evening, leaving her aunt alone in the cabin, holding onto something no one else understood.

part two

eight

The first camper arrived at 10:52 AM, carrying a small boombox and dragging a pair of exhausted-looking parents. Aunt Erin moved in quickly, taking out a list marked *Campers' Rules* and reminding the parents of rule number eight: no radios or boomboxes of any kind. Then she suggested the family tour the grounds and acquaint themselves with the facilities—refreshments could be purchased at Tuck'n Tack. Adrien sold them one package of Nibs, two Malted Milks, three Sprites and an ugly blue sweatshirt, size small.

"Haven't you got any better colors?" demanded the nine-year-old camper, pushing her glasses up her nose and glaring at the T-shirts in the display case. Adrien liked her immediately.

"The person in charge of T-shirt colors," she said, pointing, "is that lady over there."

"The one who won't let me keep my boombox?" asked the girl.

"That's the one."

"You look like her."

"Impossible," said Adrien. "I think those T-shirts are extremely ugly too."

The girl's grin was full of crooked teeth. The next time Adrien looked up, she saw her aunt receiving an earful about colors from a skinny squirt whose arms were crossed authoritatively over her chest. She would have savored the moment, but the grounds were quickly filling with campers and their families, and she was kept busy selling candy, T-shirts, buttons, postcards, calendars and datebooks, even nature-sound cassettes. Tuck'n Tack also handled the rental equipment for the mini-golf course and the volleyball court. She had just handed out the last set of clubs and was tearing open yet another container of Smarties, yelling inside her head for a five-minute break, a cigarette, The Big One, *anything* to get some relief, when she turned to serve the next person in line, and it was Roberta.

The girl was there and not there. Adrien could see her face clearly, but she was transparent as she had been in the cabin, a thin film of the past superimposed over the present tense. So were her parents, who stood in line behind her.

"I'd like a green sweatshirt." Roberta's dark hair was pulled into a short ponytail and she wore a neon pink Beatles T-shirt. Released from the photograph, her face seemed so alive, constantly on the verge of laughter, her left cheek dancing in and out of a

dimple. Her only makeup was a beauty mark drawn above her upper lip. Adrien was sure it hadn't been in the photograph. "What size d'you think, Mom?" Roberta asked, looking over her shoulder.

"Oh, large," said her mother, smiling the same dimple. "It'll shrink and god knows, you'll grow."

"And a Big Turk," Roberta said, turning back. "And a Mountain Dew. What d'you want, Shrimp?"

"I'm not a shrimp," insisted a short small voice. Leaning forward, Adrien caught sight of a four-year-old boy busily punching his older sister's leg.

"Dad, tell the jerk to stop punching me," Roberta said.

"Stop calling him names then," said her father wearily.

Another transparent family walked up behind Roberta's, and a girl with a long red ponytail leaned on the counter. "Got any Jaw Breakers?" she asked.

This girl was slightly taller than Roberta. Her face was thin, her mouth pouty. She wore heavy green eyeshadow, a familiar striped tube top, and a ring with a large stone. The two girls gave each other sideways glances while Adrien stared.

"Sherry, could you ask about T-shirts?" asked a plump red-haired woman in a flower-power dress leftover from the sixties. Her makeup left Sherry's in the dust. "For your cousin Billy's birthday, remember?"

Sherry gave her ponytail a scornful flip. "Yeah, Mom, I'm not stupid."

"I didn't say you were stupid," snapped her mother in exasperation. "And I hope this week at camp teaches you some manners. When will you learn to respect your el—"

Roberta gave Sherry a sympathetic grin, and the two girls

*tuned the adults out. "I like your mood stone," she said. "Mom
made me leave mine at home."*

*They shared eye-rolling until a mayfly landed on Sherry's
bare shoulder. "Ugh," she cried, pulling it off.*

*"Those were here last year too," said Roberta. "They stick to
you like glue, but they don't bite. They only last for a week or so,
and then they're gone. What cabin are you in?"*

"Some dork name. Prairie ... something or other."

"Sky," said Roberta.

*"More like Prairie Yawn," said Sherry. "This place is for the
dead."*

*"We'll wake it up," said Roberta. "Hey, get a T-shirt if you
can."*

"They're so ugly," complained Sherry. "Boats?!"

*"We'll decorate them," grinned Roberta. "Tie-dye in Farts
and Crafts." She blew a mouth fart on her arm.*

"Roberta, would you hurry it up?" said her father.

"See ya later, eh?" said Sherry.

"Yeah, see ya," grinned Roberta.

The girls vanished and Adrien found herself staring
into the eye sockets of a skull on a very tall T-shirt. "Gimme
a blue sweatshirt," said the living face above the skull. "And
a Mr. Big."

Even though she knew they were gone, Adrien couldn't
help leaning over the counter and scanning for the girls.
Crowds of people were coming and going, chattering in
small groups. Small children ran past in frantic bursts of
energy, and a few teenagers were bunting a ball back and
forth over the volleyball net. She felt suddenly cold. This
was how the camp must have looked to Roberta and Sherry

on their arrival day, twenty years ago—Camp Lakeshore T-shirts everywhere, children zooming around. Not the slightest sign of death.

"What're you staring at?" demanded the boy wearing the skull. "The sweatshirts are behind you, *duh*." He pulled a mayfly off his neck and held it by the wings. "What are these creepy things?"

"They're called mayflies," said Adrien, handing him a sweatshirt. "They're like large mosquitoes. They take a huge chunk out of you when they bite. Worse than horseflies."

With a yelp, the boy swiped several more off his arms.

"You owe me twenty-seven dollars and ninety-four cents," she smiled, keying it into the till. "I hope you enjoy wearing your Camp Lakeshore sweatshirt. Those boats will look lovely on you."

She was closing the awning, about to head into the dining hall for lunch, when Paul coasted up on a ten-speed. An intense flush started crawling up her neck and Adrien kicked at the wall, concentrating on the pain in her foot. "Where's your dirt bike?" she asked loudly. Making noise seemed to help.

"Come up to the corrals with me?" he asked, ignoring her question. From the look on his face, yesterday hadn't happened; they hadn't spent hours riding the wind in that long raw closeness.

"Sure," she said faintly, closing the padlock. "I just have to take the till into the office."

They rode double to the corrals, Adrien leaning back and swearing never to touch him again, but when they arrived she immediately forgot about it. "How did this happen?" she cried, running to a broken section in the fence.

"I dunno." Paul removed his baseball cap and ran a hand through his flattened hair. "It was like this when I got here. It took me over an hour to get the horses back in. They were wandering all over the woods. I just fixed this section three days ago."

"Would the horses knock it down?" Several rails had been dislodged. The nails had come out clean.

"No," he said shortly. "They scratch themselves against the fence but they don't take runs at it. Those rails weren't loose, unless I didn't nail them in properly."

The large paddock stretched back into a swampy wooded area. "Did you check over there?" she asked, pointing.

"I checked all of it," he said. "This is the only part that gave."

"I don't think it was you, Paul." She was thinking about the orienteering exercise. How many groups had seen Paul fixing this section?

"Neither do I," he said quietly. "But who could it be? And why?"

He gave her a hand and she stood. When she looked into his face this time, yesterday was there, warm and intense. For a second she wanted to stub her toe, find some way out of what she was feeling. Everything got so *hot*.

"Adrien." No one had ever said her name like that— softly, as if he was touching it. Paul's face was also flushed. His eyes flicked away, then back, and she realized he felt the same confusion. "I dreamt about you last night."

"Did you die?" she asked quickly.

"I heard you calling my name," he said, "and I woke up. You saved me."

"Good," she burst out, sudden tears in her eyes. "I saw those girls this morning, while I was working in Tuck'n Tack. They're here now. They're at camp and they're going to die. I don't want you to die too. Please stop dreaming those dreams."

"I can't stop dreaming," he said. "I dream all night. I wake up covered in sweat. I'm tired, like I haven't slept."

"Then I'm going to be in all your dreams," she said fiercely. "And I'm going to stop you from dying."

He touched her cheek and she burned a long slow fire. "I feel so many things." His eyes searched her face as if she was the last living thing. "A minute's like a year rushing past. Everything's so vivid. I've been dreaming about you for two years, and now you're here."

Tears ran down her face. She didn't know what he was telling her. "Your birthday—is it this week?"

"Soon."

"Why won't you tell me the day?"

"If you don't know," he said intensely, "it might not happen."

"You really think I can change things?"

The wind was everywhere, touching the leaves, the grass, her skin. She knew if she could do this, she could do anything, be anyone. Slowly, she reached out and traced the soft flush of his lower lip. It was like touching a dream, except it was real—she could feel the gentle give of his lip, its slight wetness. Paul closed his eyes, his breathing deepening.

"Adrien," he said. "Adrien, listen, okay?" Opening his eyes, he caught her hand and held it. "D'you remember yesterday, when my sister Michelle was talking about Leanne? Well, she was right. Leanne did dump me."

Adrien stood trapped by this change in conversation. She didn't want to hear about Leanne, she wanted to step back into her dream of touching his mouth, listening to him breathe deeper and deeper into himself.

"This is hard," Paul said hoarsely. "I've never told anyone about this, okay?"

She woke up to the fear in his eyes. A hole opened in her gut, but she nodded. He let go of her hand.

"I hurt her," he said quickly. "I didn't know it'd turn out like that, I swear. It's just—I get crazy, all this *shit* coming at me in my head. You don't know what I'm like in here." He hit his forehead with the heel of his hand. "Thinking about dying all the time, all the different ways. Thinking about missing the rest of my life. It makes me crazy to have everything now. Everything now," he said bitterly. "Mostly I hold it in, but Leanne and I were close, friends since grade four. We weren't really going out, I guess I talked her into it. She didn't really want to, I knew that." He stared off, his mouth working. "Afterwards, she wouldn't talk to me. She never talked to me again. I wrecked something for her, something important—a lot more important than what I got out of it, that's for sure." He rubbed at a trembling in his mouth, then chanced a glance at Adrien. "I'm a shit, right?"

"You're not a shit," said Adrien. "And I'm not Leanne."

Paul slumped against the fence. "Two years, I've been dreaming about you."

"It's been two years since I had my aneurysm," Adrien said slowly.

"Must mean something," he muttered. "How're you supposed to know? I don't have a fucking clue what I'm supposed to do, how I'm supposed to be. Is there some purpose to all this? Y'know, like this is the way I'm finally gonna wise up and become a better person. Well if it is, I already learned, okay? I know what an absolute jerk I can be, so until this is all over—whatever that means—everything's on hold. I'm on hold. *Life* is on hold."

"But—" said Adrien. Out in the corrals, horses wickered and nuzzled. Horses had it so easy. They didn't have to talk about it, they just did it. Words were an impossible dream. "Shit!" she erupted. "I wish I was a horse."

Paul followed her gaze out into the paddock, just as one horse began nosing the rump of another.

"Not *that* horse," she said desperately.

Paul gave a shout of laughter, then pulled his baseball cap back on. "The day after my birthday," he said, "if I'm still around, I am going into those trees. And if you come after me, we are going to build a lean-to, crawl into it and not come out for a long time."

"Why not now?" asked Adrien in a small hopeful voice.

"I'm still a crazy dying shit," Paul said simply.

It was late afternoon, the dining hall a mass of shouting, fidgeting children. As the serving line moved slowly along the counter, the hairnets dumped large helpings of sloppy joes, corn and coleslaw onto pale yellow plates. Slinking in through a side entrance, Adrien joined the closest staff table. Big mistake—they had gotten through the serving line early, and were already halfway through the mess on their plates. She had missed lunch because she had stayed at the corrals to help Paul with the fence. The hairnets had given them a few sandwiches, but now she was absolutely starved. She couldn't remember being this hungry as a camper. Buttering a slice of bread, she wolfed it down.

"So, how's little Wood?"

Connor sat across the table, mopping up the last of his sloppy joes with a piece of bread. He had spent the afternoon at the docks, putting several cabins through their waterfront orientation. Tuck'n Tack was closed on Sunday afternoons, so after the fence had been fixed, Adrien had worked at the office computer, helping Gwen slot cabins into a master activities schedule. From there, she had watched groups of children sitting on the lawn, waiting to get their medical records checked at the First Aid cabin. Beyond them, Connor had strode up and down the horizon like a bronze god, blond halo gleaming as he explained life jacket fastenings and how to hold onto a tipped canoe.

"Busy," Adrien replied.

"Now, what could keep a little girl like you busy?" he drawled, leaning back and patting his stomach.

"Fixing the fence up at the corrals. Someone vandalized it."

His eyebrows made a careful ascent. *Manufactured shock*, Adrien thought. *He's not really surprised.*

"Yeah," she continued. "It must've happened last night. Late last night. Y'know, some stupid drunks thought they'd have a good time letting out the horses."

"Sounds like the way I'd want to spend a good drunk," Connor said sarcastically.

She plunged on. "But of course, they were too drunk to unhitch the gate. Oh no, they had to take the fence apart."

"Probably some of the natives," he said easily. "Paul and his buddies."

"I don't think so!" she hissed. "More like initiation for new recruits, don't you think?"

The staff at the table had fallen completely silent. Among the shouts and laughter of several hundred children, it was an odd oasis of quiet. Hand shaking, Adrien reached for the bread basket, but Connor pulled it out of reach.

"Uh-uh," he said, smiling coldly. "Tsk-tsk."

"I don't have to play your stupid games," she said, enunciating clearly. "Midnight fire. Good times. The training manual is trash."

The staffer sitting next to Connor froze with her fork in her mouth. Even Connor had gone very still. Then a throat at the other end of the table cleared itself loudly and said, "Con, pass me that bread, would ya?"

"Sure, Bunter. Catch." Connor tossed the basket and the other guy caught it neatly, removing the last few pieces of bread.

"Sure am hungry," said Bunter, biting into all three at once.

Adrien noticed an empty seat at another staff table. She stood, about to walk over to it, but Connor caught her wrist. "Catch ya later," he said softly, tightening his grip, then letting go.

After supper, everyone filed out of the dining hall to stand in a large circle facing the flagpole. Aunt Erin was a stickler for instilling national pride—twice a day, the entire camp lined up to watch as the flag was raised or lowered. Most of the ceremony took place in complete silence, only the flag speaking into the wind. Already a camper had been selected to help Aunt Erin fold the flag—the nine-year-old squirt who had lost her boombox. Looking ridiculously serious, she stood ramrod straight at the center of the circle. It was obvious she had fallen hopelessly under the camp director's spell. Adrien could almost hear her fierce little heart beat quicker as Aunt Erin stepped forward and began a short speech.

"Tomorrow is Canada Day, a day we have set aside to honor our country and celebrate the fact that we live in a place of freedom and dignity." Adrien was surprised. She had forgotten her aunt could speak in long sentences. "This flag represents what we feel about our country and about ourselves. It stands for everything we believe in—freedom of speech, freedom to worship …"

Five girls stepped forward and stood around the flagpole in a small group. It was early morning, the horizon lit with first light. At the top of the flagpole flew a single pair of girl's panties.

"I told Mom!" wailed Roberta. "They stole all of them. That's the only pair I have left and they stuck it up there." She stood, hands on hips, looking very pleased as she watched her pink panties flutter.

"Bet you they're wearing the rest of them," observed Sherry.

"No way!" gawked a girl with a long tumble of brown hair who was standing beside her.

"You don't want them back, Roberta," advised Nat. "They'll be stretched way out of shape." She made a lewd gesture and the girls burst into fidgety laughter.

"What'm I gonna wear?" demanded Roberta.

"Nothing," grinned Nat. "None of us will, for the whole week. But don't tell Erin, okay? Only us'll know."

"No underwear?" The fifth girl looked shocked.

"C'mon, Cath, this is your big chance to dump those bloomers your mother makes you wear." Quickly Nat unzipped her shorts, stepped out of them, removed her panties and pulled her shorts back on. "Hooey!" she cried, waving her panties over her head. "Everyone do it!"

"Someone'll see," protested Cath, looking around.

"Everyone's asleep. Erin's snoring and you know why." Nat began to dance around the flagpole.

"I dunno," said Cath, but the other girls were following suit, sitting down to tug off their jeans.

"My bum's wet from the dew," laughed Roberta as she scrambled to her feet.

"You've got a bug on it," Sherry observed.

Delicately, Roberta removed the mayfly, then pulled her jeans back on. "Yahoo!" Waving her panties over her head, she joined Nat in the dance around the flagpole. Soon the others joined in, giggling and snorting through a wobbly version of "O Canada". Finally Sherry stopped dancing and stood staring upward. Her face held a look of awe.

"Let's put them all up there," she whispered fiercely.

Adrien watched the bright red maple leaf descend in small jerks, sagging as it came out of the wind. Then Aunt Erin and her nine-year-old fan were folding the flag and putting it into its overnight box. Serious faces began singing "O Canada" as a V of geese flew across the lake. Adrien mouthed the words, but their meaning escaped her. She couldn't believe what she had just seen. Every summer she had stood in line, morning and evening, listening to her aunt's speeches, watching the red leaf and believing in its holiness. Now for one vivid moment, she saw six pairs of pink and white panties flying wildly at the top of the flagpole, catching the light as the morning sun rose over the lake.

She would never be the same again.

nine

She was jerked roughly out of sleep, into the glare of a flashlight. Once again, her blankets were pulled off the bed. This time she backed into the wall, shielding her eyes.

"You've broken a long tradition, Grouch."

Connor was speaking in a deep unfamiliar voice, but she recognized him. What made him think he could pretend to be a different person at night? And why did everyone else pretend along with him? Even Darcie stood in the shadows, ready to jump at his slightest command.

"I don't like your traditions," she said. "No one made them the law."

"They're the law here." He pulled her hand from her face. She blinked and tried to turn her head. "Bad girls have to be punished, you know."

"What're you, a bunch of Nazis?"

He snapped his fingers and two guys leaned toward her—the waterfront assistant and one of the riding instructors. They grabbed her arms and pulled her off the bed.

"C'mon," said Connor, leaving the room. She was pushed toward the door, then forced along the hall. As they emerged outside, she started to yell, and a hand was clamped over her mouth. The flashlight was so close, she could feel its heat on her face.

"Make another sound and it'll get worse," Connor said quietly.

She fell silent. They weren't really hurting her—if she didn't struggle, they held her quite loosely. The procession wound its way through the trees, past the dining hall and the office, then on toward the corrals until it reached the Petting Zoo, a small fenced-in enclosure that housed two sheep, one goat and several rabbits. Every day, the youngest campers came here to feed and pet the animals. As Connor vaulted the fence, the sheep bleated sleepily and backed away.

"Pass her over," he said.

The fence was no more than a meter high. She kicked and struggled, but was easily lifted into his waiting arms. His breath stank of beer and his chin stubble rubbed her cheek, but when she pushed against his chest, he tightened his grip. He carried her effortlessly. Several more figures leapt into the enclosure.

"Darcie, get your ass in here," Connor ordered.

With assistance, Darcie climbed the fence.

"Open it up," Connor said.

As Darcie took out a key, someone trained the flashlight on the small cage in one corner of the pen that housed the animals' feed. With a start, Adrien remembered that one of her roommate's additional duties was the Petting Zoo's early morning feeding.

"I don't really think we should—" Darcie began, but Connor cut her off.

"Maybe we'll put you in instead?"

Darcie unlocked the cage. "It's too full," she said. "Grouch won't fit."

"So pull out a bale," said Connor.

Hands pulled out the closest bale of hay.

"Great," said Connor. "Lots of room. In you go, Grouch. Sit in the cage where all the bad animals belong."

She tried to hang onto the doorframe, but they pressed her arms to her sides and shoved her through. The small door closed, the padlock clicked shut, and the staff moved in to circle the cage. She counted eleven shapes shifting nervously in the dark.

"Erin Wood," Connor said, and everyone stomped and grunted. Adrien crouched in the cage and waited. "So, little Wood," Connor sneered. "How d'you like your new home?"

She couldn't believe the snickers. They had to be completely drunk, too drunk to see her shaking. "Oh, I'm really scared," she said. "The sheep might tear the cage apart and eat me alive. In the morning, my aunt'll find me and you'll be fired."

"Then maybe we'd better make sure no one finds you." Connor crouched by the cage and flicked a lighter. The small flame cast flickering shadows across the bales.

"What're you doing?" gasped Darcie.

"Shut up." Connor held the flame under several wisps of hay sticking through the wire mesh. "You gonna tell your auntie, Grouch?"

"I didn't say I was going to tell," Adrien said nervously. "I said she'd find me in the morning if you left me here all night."

"Oh, we wouldn't do that," Connor said soothingly. "Not *all* night, Grouch."

The hay caught fire and flames shot inward.

"No!" Darcie shoved Connor aside and began stomping the flames with her shoe. As quickly as the fire had flared, it died. "What d'you think you're doing?" she hissed.

"Just testing your loyalties."

"You can't *kill* people," Darcie cried. "That's not part of any camp tradition."

"No one was going to kill her." Connor spoke calmly. "And you interfered."

"But—" Darcie stammered.

"We're finished for tonight," said Connor. "Beddy-bye for all good staffies. C'mon, Darcie." He took her by the shoulders and pushed her toward the fence. Then he and the others vaulted it, leaving her standing alone, staring at the wire mesh. Connor played the flashlight over her face. Everyone watched her take a deep breath, as if coming awake.

"This is stupid," Darcie said. "I've got the key." She walked to the pen's main gate, unlocked it and stepped out. "See ya later, Grouch," she whispered, then joined the others as they headed toward their cabins. The rustling of leaves faded. There was the distant snapping of a twig, then enormous silence. Adrien's heart beat bright stars across the sky.

"This shit only works if everyone believes it," she yelled into the looming dark, then slumped against the cage door. She couldn't believe they were actually leaving her here.

"On Canada Day," she muttered. "Country of freedom and dignity. Freedom of expression and all that."

The goat was nibbling her hair. Adrien twisted the loose strands into a tight braid and tucked it into her collar. She was dressed for bed in her usual T-shirt and panties, and the mosquitoes were swarming. Bales crowded her into the door, and the top of her head pushed against the mesh roof. More mesh pressed against her back and bare feet. How could Darcie do this? Tears stung Adrien's eyes and throat. Some friend. Some Spartan. Darcie was just like everyone else, kissing Connor's ass. Roberta would never have gone along with this shit. Sherry wouldn't have believed in it. Nat would have told Connor to kiss his own ass. Adrien smiled a little. Or hers.

It was so quiet. Everyone was asleep. Were they planning to leave her here all night? What if The Big One hit? It would serve them right if they found her dead in the morning—explain that one to Aunt Erin. She lifted a bare foot and kicked against the mesh. It belled out but held firm. She kicked again, the mesh cutting into her skin. "Ouch." She didn't want to wreck the cage, but they had no *right*. Did they expect her to sit quietly until someone came to let her out? Roberta wouldn't. Nat would tear the cage apart with her bare hands.

"I want out!" Adrien yelled, banging the mesh with

her fist. Pain laced her skin, followed by a surge of anger, and she punched the mesh again. There was no way she was going to sit here waiting obediently for Connor's return. "Let me out!" She got onto her knees, head pressed against the roof, fist pounding in a regular rhythm. Rage rose in her throat, filled her head, and raw words tore out of her. "I could die, don't you know I could die? I've got a fucked-up brain. It could explode and I'd die out here all alone. It's not my fault. I didn't ask for a defective brain or weak blood vessels. I didn't ask to eat dirt and shit my pants. I used to be like the rest of you and then my life fell apart. I hate being me. I hate me. Let me out."

Darcie was suddenly there in the dark, fumbling with the key, unlocking the cage door and taking her arm. "All right, okay, take it easy, would ya? I was just waiting until they were gone. Shh, you'll wake your aunt. Jesus, what'd you do to your hand?"

Adrien crawled out and stood shaking as her roommate shone a small flashlight over her puffy right hand. It was lacerated with small cuts. "Crap," Darcie muttered. "I'm so sorry, Grouch. I'm so sorry." Before Adrien could move, Darcie wrapped her in a bear hug. Soft and warm, it was full of beating hearts, something to bring her back from the end of the world, the end of herself. "Shh," Darcie whispered. "Shh, shh." Her hair grew soggy from Adrien's tears. "That's all right," Darcie soothed. "That's okay."

The goat started chewing Adrien's T-shirt. She kicked at it and the two girls pulled apart, wiping away tears. "Grouch," Darcie asked hesitantly. "You were yelling something … about your brain? Dying? What—?"

"I had a brain aneurysm," Adrien gulped, staring off into the dark. "Two years ago. If it happens again, I'm gone. I was just lucky the first time."

"Oh." Darcie turned off the flashlight. "Your aunt didn't tell me."

"My aunt," Adrien said scornfully, "pretends everything's normal. It's my attitude that's the problem. She probably thinks my attitude caused the first one."

"I doubt it." The warmth of Darcie's hand closed around Adrien's good one. "C'mon, Grouch. Let's go home."

Adrien smiled a little. One week in a cabin and her roommate called it home. Everywhere Darcie went, home went too. Darcie was her own home. She dropped Adrien's hand to unlock the outer gate, then took it again firmly, leading her into the trees like a child.

An image was growing in Adrien's mind—cool, quiet, whispering with hidden meanings. A place moonlight touched the earth and rooted, going so deep it became darkness. Two halves that connected to form a whole. Her home. She turned, taking Darcie with her, leading her toward the lake.

"Where are we going?" Darcie asked. "I have to fix your hand. I'm tired, I want—"

"Shh." They were almost at another clearing. Small pale shapes could be seen through the trees. Darcie took a quick breath, then went quiet. They crept closer and watched. It was one of the youngest cabins—the seven-year-olds. The girls wore sweatshirts and jackets over their nighties, and were clustered around their counselor in a small awed group, listening.

"It's older than any of us, even me. It's older than your grandma or your great-grandma. This tree is older than any of the animals or buildings here at Camp Lakeshore."

"Older than the sea?" asked a girl, pointing in the direction of the lake.

"Almost," said the counselor. "This tree is very very old and it's very very wise."

"How'd it get so smart?" asked another girl.

"Cuz it got struck by lightning. Then you're extra smart," said a third.

"Then you're extra dead," said the first.

"Not this tree," said the counselor. "This is the Wishing Tree and it lives just to hear the wishes of children. D'you think it's going to let some dumb ol' lightning come along and kill it?"

"No," chorused the girls.

Adrien's throat tightened and she blinked fiercely.

"The Wishing Tree is going to hear all your wishes tonight," the counselor continued. "All you have to do is touch the tree and tell it your most secret wish."

"Do I have to say it out loud?" asked a small voice.

"This tree is so wise, it can hear the softest thought whispered inside your head," said the counselor. "It can hear what no one else can hear. When you're ready, just put your hand on the trunk and wish like this." She closed her eyes and stood for a long poised moment, one hand pressed against the white bark. Then she opened her eyes, smiled and stepped back.

"Did the Wishing Tree hear you?" asked a girl.

"Oh yes," said the counselor.

"Good," the girl said fervently. One by one, each child stepped forward and touched the tree, most of them imitating their counselor's pose. One hugged the tree, another stooped to touch the fallen part. When they were finished, the counselor had them all join hands.

"Now the Wishing Tree knows your wish. Each leaf on these branches holds someone's wish. The Wishing Tree never forgets a wish. Now your wish is up there among the leaves, blowing in the wind." The girls stood open-mouthed, listening to the tree rustle until their counselor took the nearest girl's hand and led them back to their cabin.

"That's Tamai," sighed Darcie. "Isn't she neat? She missed staff training, but this is her fourth summer, so she doesn't need it. She always counsels the youngest girls."

"They need her," Adrien said hoarsely. She stepped into the clearing and stood looking at the tree. The moon was partially covered, but the trunk still glowed, a shadowy light with a dark burn slash. Leaves on the fallen half were starting to brown. Part of its life was leaving. Adrien walked to the tree and placed both hands on the standing half. "C'mere, Spart."

She needed to say this out loud, and she needed someone to hear it. Darcie stepped close, her sleeve brushing Adrien's bare arm. For a moment, the Wishing Tree seemed to pause. Its leaves stopped rustling and the air held silent, waiting.

"I want," Adrien said softly, "to know about death. How long it takes for the heart to stop beating. When do you stop knowing? What happens when you lose yourself? Does all the light shooting through your brain go out quick like a bedroom light, or does it unravel slow, like a sweater, giving you time? Does the throat clutch up? Can you get out that last important word? How cold will my skin feel? Will I feel it turning cold, or will I already be gone? Will my eyes turn blue? How blue? Will I see only blue things then, only sky? I want to know if you rise up and blow with the wind, or if you sink down, far down into cold water, nothing closes over your face, nothing is all you are, all you ever were."

She knelt and touched the dying half. "And I want to know about life. What it's like to truly believe in it. Because life only works if you believe in it, right Spart?"

"Right," whispered Darcie.

"So I want to believe in it," said Adrien, waiting, and the cool green sensation came through her, washing her clean. She breathed deeply and stood. "That's my wish— two wishes, but they're the same wish. What's yours?"

Darcie's face was a mess of tears. "I want to be the best friend you've ever had."

Adrien was suddenly very tired and needed her roommate's hand to make it back to the cabin. The short walk seemed interminable. When they finally stumbled into the cabin, the rest of the staff were asleep. Darcie took out a first-aid kit and cleaned Adrien's hand. "What's your aunt going to say about this?" she sighed. "Every time you're around me, you get bashed up. I'm so gutless. I never should've let them put you in that cage. I'm telling you something now, Grouch. I am not going to that campfire ever again. I'm staying in bed and getting a good night's sleep. Connor'll be mad, but it's true what you said—shit only works if you believe in it. If you can stand up to him, so can I." She looked grimly determined, as if her life stood in the balance.

"So you disobey them." Adrien climbed into bed. "What can they do about it? Their big punishment was to lock me in the Petting Zoo."

Darcie's eyes turned vague. "Oh, they do things," she said. "A lot of bullying. Hazing. Every night, there's some victim. If you don't join in, you become the victim. Everyone's so eager not to be the next victim."

"I thought it was just good times," Adrien said faintly.

"It used to be," said Darcie. "It wasn't like this last year, when I worked on maintenance. A guy named Ernie led the campfires then. He kept it cool, just a place staff could go for a beer. You didn't have to go every night and there wasn't any hazing. I guess it depends on who leads it. Connor was here last year too, doing that grunt thing about your aunt, but it was a just a fun thing then. Not mean like now."

"It was always mean," said Adrien. "He just wasn't in charge."

"Yeah, I guess," Darcie said softly. "I guess we let him take over and change things." She took a deep breath. "Well, I'm not going back. We'll stick together, Grouch. What can they do to us if we stick together?"

Adrien turned out the light. "Maybe they should start worrying about what we could do to them."

"What could we do?"

"Ask the Wishing Tree in your dreams. Maybe we'll know by morning."

ten

She was floating just under the water's surface, curled into herself. The rhythm of the water was the rhythm of breathing; she rose and fell on the water's breathing as if it was forever, as if all things could be like this, at peace, waiting for the heart to speak. Slowly, Adrien's eyes opened. Darcie's bed was empty—she was probably getting rid of last night's evidence at the Petting Zoo. Adrien rolled and stretched. In spite of missed sleep, she felt soft and warm, full of small yawns. She knew she had to decide what to do about Connor, but it was difficult to worry with all this gentleness in her body. The person she really wanted to think about was Paul—she had to talk to him this morning, find out what he had dreamed about, if he had lived or died, and how. And she had to *make* him tell his birth date, when it was coming, if it was today.

It could be today. Heartbeat quickening, she showered, then headed to the dining hall. For once she was early. Maybe the hairnets would give her some toast and jam before everyone else came in. If she learned how to say please in their weird language, they might even cook her an ecstatic omelet. She was opening the door to the kitchen, about to go in and beg, when the sound of whispering caught her ear and she turned to find herself in sudden darkness.

A crescent moon glimmered overhead, and five girls glided past the dining hall into the trees. They were obviously trying to keep quiet—Cath giggled and was immediately shushed—and they seemed intent on something just ahead of them.

"Can you still see her?" Sherry whispered to Roberta, who led the way. The five were dressed in nighties and baby dolls. No one had bothered to pull on a sweatshirt.

Roberta nodded. "This is the same way she came last night. I followed her about this far, and then I lost her."

"She sure ain't going to the can," observed Nat.

They were headed toward the campfire. It was a different route and there were no white ribbons tied to the trees, but Adrien recognized the area.

"Why would Erin come out here in the middle of the night?" whispered the girl with the long tumble of brown hair.

"Shh," hissed Sherry and Roberta.

Fire flickered through the bush, and the sound of laughter drifted toward the girls. Ahead, the trees opened and a figure stepped from the path into the clearing, pausing so that her wheat-blond hair caught the firelight in a sudden halo. Friendly cries greeted the young Erin Wood, and a guy put his arm around her. Someone gave a soft whistle as they kissed.

"Peter Pecker," whispered Nat with satisfaction.

Adrien had been so intent on watching her aunt that she had forgotten the girls. She seemed to have crept in among them, and was surrounded as they crouched together in the dark.

"I told you she was meeting him!" Nat was triumphant. "Bet you they don't stay here long."

Before Nat finished her sentence, Erin and the young man had turned and were walking into the trees. "C'mon," hissed Roberta, and the girls crept after the pair. The couple didn't go far. He spread a blanket and they lay down together. Hidden among the trees, the girls' breathing took on a quick short rhythm, their eyes beady and shameless, watching in stunned amazement as clothing came loose, and bodies were naked and joined. The guy kept whispering Erin's name, but she seemed to lose all words, the sounds she made, almost singing.

Something rose in Adrien then, too huge to be understood, though she felt it—emotions that swirled like a storm. She was lost in it, turned from what she had seen, what her aunt kept hidden and never let show. Running, she felt like she was running through trees in the dark, stumbling over roots, branches whipping her face, but when she could think again, she found herself still standing beside the west kitchen entrance, as if she had never moved. The early morning sun slanted down to touch and warm her, the trees heaved in a slow breeze. She couldn't get the young Erin Wood's small joyous cries out of her head.

She continued to hear them through flag-raising and her aunt's Canada Day speech. She joined the staff breakfast line still trying to shake the wildness that echoed through her. The assistant director was up front, organizing the entry into the dining hall. Fortunately, Aunt Erin had disappeared—Adrien was sure her constant stare would have bored away sections of her aunt's head.

Darcie stepped out of her position further up the line and walked back to her. "What's wrong, Grouch?"

Adrien shrugged. Other staff were watching them closely. Darcie hadn't been seen talking to her since early last week. "Did you clean up the Petting Zoo?"

Darcie nodded. "Should we tell your aunt?"

Adrien shot Connor a glance. He was at the front of the line, joking with other staff. Last night seemed to be forgotten, a trivial event. She thought of what it had meant to her. She had won, really. She had opened cages Connor knew nothing about. "Y'know," she said slowly, "the whole thing was just *so* stupid."

"Yeah?" Darcie asked dubiously.

"So act like it," Adrien shrugged. "If Aunt Erin asks, I was running and I fell on my hand. You bandaged it, right?"

The two girls looked at each other, understanding creeping across Darcie's face. She glanced at Connor. "He isn't worth it, is he, Grouch?"

"He ain't worth half a sneeze."

Her roommate nodded again. "For the first time this summer, I didn't crawl out of bed like a slug. And I'm going to sleep all night tonight. Just think of how tomorrow's going to be."

"Maybe you'll even have time to curl that Spartan hair of yours."

Darcie gave a small shriek and covered her hair with her hands. "I forgot!"

"You missed your face too."

"My makeup," whispered Darcie.

Adrien grinned. "Robin Hood would be proud."

The maintenance crew held a daily 8:30 meeting at the east kitchen entrance. Adrien sat on the steps, watching for Paul's bike. She was the only staff who didn't have to be at her post until 9 AM. Maybe her aunt was going easy on her. Maybe she did give a thought to stressed-out blood vessels. Most of the maintenance crew had assembled and were listening to Guy's instructions. Paul didn't actually clean toilets—he was usually repairing something—but he met with the rest of them, and he was usually early. Adrien stood and walked over to the group. "Guy, d'you know where Paul is?"

He gave her a knowing grin. "Miss him already, eh?"

She took a quick breath, trying to beat the flush rising in her face. "I just have to talk to him."

"Probably on his way," said Guy. "But get your smooching in quick. We're driving up to Ranch Camp to stock up supplies."

Ranch Camp was a program for advanced horseback riders that was located at a separate campsite, a two-hour drive from Camp Lakeshore. Adrien headed for the office and caught the screen door just as it was swinging into place behind her aunt. "When is Paul's birthday?" she demanded. "Today?"

Aunt Erin gave her a very blue glance. "He'll tell you if he wants to."

"You don't understand." Adrien's voice rose in frustration. "I have to know."

"Boy has a right to keep personal information to himself." Her aunt picked up the phone.

"I hate you!" Adrien stomped her foot.

"Mentioned that already." Aunt Erin began dialing. It was an old phone, had probably been sitting on the desk since the '70s—a relic from the past, just like her aunt. That cold distant woman sitting in front of her couldn't possibly connect to the teenager Adrien had just heard, giving those uncontrolled cries of wonder in the woods.

"Your clock stopped again," Adrien said. "1:37, just like last time."

Aunt Erin seemed to stop breathing. "First cabin comes by Tuck'n Tack at 9:30," she said, fixing the clock. "Best be ready."

Adrien heard the faint whir of a ten-speed. She whirled and ran out, letting the screen door slam. "Paul!" she yelled. He braked, then turned and coasted to a stop in front of her. Beneath the tan, his face was pale. Dark smudges shadowed his eyes.

"What's the matter?" she asked. "Why're you late?"

He slumped forward, resting his forehead on the handlebars. "Michelle had to go visit some puppies down the road. I biked her there first."

She felt stupid with relief and stared at the curl of hair at the nape of his neck. She wanted to touch it, curl it around her finger ... and then she was. Her hand floated strangely through the air, hovered above his neck, then picked up the dark curl and played with it. Sweet heat rushed her face—she heard soft cries coming from the woods. She let go of Paul's hair and stood looking at her hand as if it belonged to someone else, someone who could touch those kinds of feelings and hold them close.

He turned his head and rested it on his arms, smiling up at her. She took a deep breath and smiled back. "What'd you dream about?"

His smile vanished. "I don't want to talk about it."

"But you have to tell me," she said. "They're my dreams too."

"No, they're not." Paul started to turn his bike, but she stepped in front of him, trapping the wheel between her legs.

"If I'm in them," she said, "they're mine."

Reluctantly, he laughed. "You're as bad as I am."

She gripped the handlebars with both hands. "I'm not moving until you tell me."

His eyes were heavy with fatigue. "It was both of us this time."

"How?"

"It doesn't matter. The method's always changing."

"I want to know."

Paul's eyes flinched, then held steady. "We were in a boat with Connor. He tipped it and we were both going down when I woke up."

"Did Connor?"

"I didn't notice."

The office door opened and Aunt Erin stepped out. "Morning, Paul."

"Sorry I'm late. I had to double-ride Michelle to the neighbor's."

Aunt Erin nodded. Paul gave a gentle tug at his bike but Adrien hung on, resisting her aunt's unspoken order. "Where's your dirt bike?"

"I don't take it to work," he said. "Could get ripped off."

Adrien watched as he rode toward the kitchen, ignoring her aunt's pointed silence. Finally she turned to see the screen door being held wide open. "Put out extra T-shirts," said her aunt. "Kids always go for T-shirts on their second day at camp."

Adrien passed under her aunt's arm and through the doorway. "It's a tradition, right?"

"Took the words right out of my mouth," said her aunt, coming in behind her.

All morning long, children filed past, pointing to Big Turks or Coffee Crisps, ordering the occasional T-shirt. Cards had been filled out for each camper, listing their spending money. Adrien was kept busy calculating the amount spent, then deducting it from the card. Two or three cabins were scheduled per half hour, so it was steady but not frenetic. Tamai came through at 10:30, a row of seven-year-olds following her like ducklings. The first child was shyly requesting a package of Reese's Pieces when Connor jogged up and threw out an order for Smarties. The row of ducklings twisted to look at him, wide-eyed.

"Smarties," Connor said again, stepping forward.

Adrien remembered the little girls touching the Wishing Tree, telling it their secrets. She leaned over the counter and gently tapped the first girl on the top of her head. "I think you were interrupted," she said. "Here at Tuck'n Tack, everyone waits their turn. Now, what did you wish to order?"

"Reese's Pieces," the girl whispered.

"Reese's Pieces. My favorite," said Adrien. "Here you are, one package of Reese's Pieces." She looked at the next girl. "And what would you like?"

The girl thought fiercely. "I want an Oh Henry! No, a Smarties, no, a, um, I don't know what I want. I think maybe a Smar—Ni—Mr.— Oh, I know, a root beer."

"Thirsty, eh?" said Adrien. She handed the child a root beer.

"I'm in a hurry," snapped Connor.

"I'm not," said Adrien. She took extreme care listening to each child's request, then looked at Tamai. "And what would you like?" The ducklings clustered around their counselor, leaning against her as they carefully unwrapped their treats. Tamai ruffled their hair, one after the other, making sure she touched each one.

"I said I'm in a hurry," Connor blustered.

"I didn't hear you, Tamai," said Adrien.

"I've got a class waiting!" said Connor.

"I think," said Tamai, thinking aloud slowly … very slowly, Adrien noted. "I'll have a Caramilk. No wait—Nibs."

"Sure about that?" asked Adrien.

"Yeah, today it'll be the Nibs." They gave each other wide-open smiles.

"Now where did those Nibs get to?" Adrien puttered around the display case.

"Here." Connor stabbed the counter top with his finger.

"What d'you know?" said Adrien. "Right in their cage

where they belong." She handed the package to Tamai, who gave one last satisfied smile and herded her ducklings away.

"Why is he so mad?" a small voice demanded loudly.

"Oh, he's just grumpy," said Tamai. "We're not grumpy, are we?"

"No," chorused the ducklings.

Adrien couldn't wipe the grin off her face. "What can I do for you, Grouch?"

Connor's face burned a slow red. "Smarties, smart ass."

"Here you are," she said brightly. "Have a nice day."

He stepped closer and spoke quickly. "I saw Darcie let you out. You think I really would've left you there all night? I was just about to let you out myself when she showed up."

She watched him fidget nervously with the Smarties package. "You didn't have the key," she said. "Darcie had it."

His eyes flickered. "I would've gone and gotten her. That's just what I was going to do when she showed up and got you out."

A cabin of boys rounded the corner. Eight-year-olds crowded in around Connor and plastered their faces to the display case. Their counselor paused behind them, glancing from Connor to Adrien.

"Who's first?" Adrien asked. There was a chorus of "Me, me, me!" Abruptly, Connor jogged off. Adrien felt as if she had been unplugged from an electrical circuit. The relief that flooded her almost dropped her to the floor.

"You all right?" The counselor pushed through the boys and leaned over the counter. "You're awfully pale."

She laid her face on the counter and let the dizziness pass. "Yeah, sure. I'm okay."

The counselor ordered his shoving, yapping group into a line and turned back to her. "I heard about what happened last night. I wasn't there because I'm a counselor, but I can tell you—most of us don't like it."

"You don't?" Adrien stared.

"No." The counselor looked around uneasily, as if expecting Connor or Bunter to leap out at him. He wore glasses and looked like the studious type. "Staff are talking. They're pissed off. The whole thing's getting out of hand."

The boy waiting at the head of the line gave the counselor a shove. The counselor shoved him back. "Wait your turn. I'm first. I'll take an Oh Henry! and a Coke."

"Stop going to the campfire," Adrien said as she handed him the candy. "Let Connor sit there by himself."

"I don't have to go while I've got this rat pack," said the counselor, "but I rotate to maintenance next week." He turned and glared at the squirming line of boys. "Would you rodents keep quiet for one second?" The boys made terrified faces and froze, staring at him. The counselor gave a heavy sigh and turned back to her. "I'll think about it," he said. "Everyone's thinking about it, actually."

It was as if the day changed colors. It had never occurred to Adrien that everyone might secretly be on her side. Slightly stunned, she watched the weary counselor lead his yapping pack toward the mini-golf course. Somehow she had forgotten the most important thing. Staff weren't robots. Each one had a free-thinking mind, and it looked as if some of them might start using it.

On her fifteen-minute break, she used the office phone to call home and wish her parents a happy Canada Day. Her mother answered. For some inexplicable reason, Adrien felt as if they hadn't spoken in years. They talked in rushes, their voices weaving in and out of each other. "I'm okay," Adrien kept saying. "Everything's fine, I'm not over-exerting myself. Aunt Erin has me on the easiest schedule of anyone."

She didn't know how to get past her mother's questions to tell her, *Something's changing, Mom. Something deep and sleepy inside me is starting to wake up.* So she just said, "I fell and cut my hand, but my roommate Darcie fixed it. My roommate's the archery instructor. She hits a bull's eye every single time."

She said good-bye three times before her mother let her go. Then she stood, one hand resting on the phone, letting the latest truth settle in. The phone call had been good. For the first time in two years, she had wanted to talk to her mother. Their voices had merged and run together—she couldn't remember half of what they had said. What stayed with her was the feel of her mother's voice, the tone of it—the love her mother felt for her, the love she felt back. At home in Saskatoon, she knew her mother was probably crying with relief. When she finished, she might relax and breathe a little deeper, smile a few times. Perhaps she would even be able to let the day be more than constant worry, the sickening lurch of fear.

Aunt Erin turned from the computer and looked at her. "How's your mom?"

Adrien had forgotten her aunt was in the office. She stared out the window as hundreds of tiny hooks let go and slipped out of her. How she had worried about her mother.

"She's good," she said slowly. "I think she'll be all right."

Aunt Erin's smile changed her whole face. "Glad to hear it," she said. "Think I'll ever get my sweatshirt back?"

"Maybe if the Tories get re-elected."

Aunt Erin grimaced. "She can keep it. Now head on out there, you've got kids waiting."

"Yes, boss," Adrien said, and stepped out to serve the children.

eleven

As Adrien was closing Tuck'n Tack for lunch, Darcie came by with a large paper bag. "Din-din," she said, shaking it. "I told the cooks you were helping me fix arrows."

"And they bought it?"

"Well, you are." With a menacing look, Darcie picked up the whistle she wore around her neck.

Adrien covered her ears and cowered. "Not the whistle, not the whistle."

They passed a group of children coming back from the corrals, but otherwise it was a quiet walk through rustling trees. The range was empty, just the equipment shed at one end and the targets at the other. Adrien snooped through the bag while Darcie unlocked the shed and brought out a canister of damaged arrows.

"Beans," Adrien announced, opening two warm Tupperware containers. "It's Canada Day and they give us sausages and beans."

"Glad I'm working out here all afternoon." Darcie sat down beside her. "Can you imagine being cooped up with a pack of little farts in Arts and Crafts?"

"Farts and Crafts," said Adrien, remembering. They dug into their beans. "This must be the cheapest way to feed a couple hundred kids."

"Yeah, but it's healthy," said Darcie. "Maybe it'll improve their brain activity. One idiot was tearing the feathers off an arrow this morning. Complete barbarian."

"Did you blow your whistle?"

"I blew his head off. You'd think kids would have some appreciation for the finesse of this sport. It's supposed to be quiet and peaceful. Zennish, like meditation. The power of the mind—"

"—over a circle pinned to a straw bale," finished Adrien. Darcie developed a distinctly huffy quality about the mouth. "You've got very nice trees around here," Adrien continued hastily. "Lovely atmosphere for mind over matter stuff."

Darcie gave her a suspicious glance, then decided to give her the benefit of the doubt. "You should see the professional ranges."

"That what you're going to be when you grow up—a professional Robin Hood?"

"I'm not good enough. I can hit a straw bale, but ... What're you going to do?"

"You mean if I don't keel over first?" Adrien had never given much thought to a professional career. "Maybe I'll work in a funeral home. Become a mortician. Find out how everything looks inside, how each organ works to keep you alive."

"I don't know if that'd really suit you, Grouch," Darcie said carefully. "They don't allow a sense of humor in funeral homes. You'd have to ditch all your snappy comebacks. Why not work in a nursery, with itty-bitty newborn babies? That'd teach you a lot more about how the body's alive, wouldn't it?"

Adrien sat watching the trees play with shadow and light. She had never held a baby. What would it be like to hold a tiny life that didn't even know it was possible to die? "You think different from me," she said grudgingly.

Darcie scraped up the last of her beans. "Yeah, but I'm a limited thinker compared to you. I can tell. You've got the kind of mind that travels to other planets, like the Doomsday Man."

"Paul Marchand?"

"You're blushing," Darcie said softly. "It's okay, I already know you're crazy about him."

Adrien wanted to scramble to her feet and *leave*. Why did everyone have to tease—was it the summer camp mentality? "Promise you won't ever bug me about this," she said, staring fiercely at a bull's eye.

"Yeah sure," Darcie said easily. "Cross my heart, hope to—"

"Die," Adrien said, looking at her. Darcie's eyes faltered, and then she nodded. "Have you ever had a boyfriend?"

Darcie switched to the non-death topic with relief. "Yeah, a couple. Not all at once, of course."

"So, uh, how far did you go?"

Darcie looked startled. "You mean sex?"

Adrien nodded.

"I've never had sex. Yet. Came pretty close a few times, but that's as far as I wanted to go. It has to be right, y'know. You have to feel right about it. It's important, letting some-one touch you." She paused. "You and Paul haven't—"

"No." Adrien shook her head. "It's just … it feels so *strong*. Like if we just kissed, we'd go all the way, y'know?"

Darcie smiled knowingly. "Yeah, but it's not like that. Feelings are strong, but you've still got a mind. You can take it in stages. Have fun with it. Play."

"Have fun?" Adrien was stunned. *Play?* The whole thing seemed so serious, almost like a pact with death.

"Look, Grouch," said Darcie. "You're going to have a ton of boyfriends. I can tell. You'll have a lot more than me. Paul's a nice guy, but you're not *marrying* him—just making out."

How could she possibly explain to Darcie what was going on between Paul and herself? "I just really like him."

"You go all gooey every time you see him."

"I do?" Adrien was horrified.

"So does he," Darcie soothed. "He sees you and he loses his knees. Don't worry, it happens to everyone. Now, see this arrow here? This is how you glue a feather onto a shaft. Are you watching carefully, Grouch?"

"Yeah, I'm watching," said Adrien. "But I'm not fixing any of your precious arrows, Spart. I can't concentrate. I'm getting hot flashes."

"That bad, eh?"

"Yeah."

"So next time you see him," Darcie advised breezily, "jump him."

All afternoon, she handed out this-or-that chocolate bar. All afternoon, she sat with her head cocked, listening for the sound of Guy's pickup coming down the road. Time stretched, endless as the horizon across the lake. By the time the pickup finally pulled into the parking lot, everyone had gone into the dining hall for supper. Adrien rushed to the walkway and watched Paul climb out of the truck.

"C'mon in and get some supper before you head home," said Guy. "Hey—Paul!"

Paul was standing, one hand on the pickup's fender, staring at Adrien. She stared back. Guy removed his black cowboy hat and shook his head. "He's all yours," he said, coming toward Adrien. "Been thinking about you all day. Must be true love—couldn't get a word out of him."

He walked away, leaving the two of them watching each other over the pickup. "Can we go for a smoke?" Adrien asked. "Or d'you want to get some supper?"

He shook his head, then said quietly, "I should get my bike."

They walked silently into the woods, the whir of the bike between them. She felt hollow and hungry, and wondered what they were having for supper. Paul leaned his bike against a tree and dug for his pack in the pocket of his lumber jacket. When she shook her head, his hand froze. She stepped toward him. Close. Closer. She could see the pores in his skin, the tiny creases in his lips. Warmth flowed through her, she wanted to touch him, she wanted—

"Whoa!" Paul stepped back, wiping sweat from his upper lip. "C'mon, Adrien. I told you—my head's too crazy right now. Don't bug me. " Grabbing his bike, he swung it onto the path. Then he mounted and pedaled off, leaving her standing alone in the shock of her skin.

She wandered the woods for hours, drifting with the dying light, touching the bark of trees. *Adrien—don't bug me. Don't bug me.* Just this morning, she had touched his hair and he had smiled up at her. She could remember the exact curve to his lips, the lines at the corner of his mouth. Where had that smile gone now, how had she made him change, what had she done wrong? Sick with a deep ache, she couldn't imagine seeing him again, walking toward him, talking to him. Stupid, she had been so stupid, and Darcie and Guy had been wrong. Paul didn't love her, no one loved her, she would die before anyone ever did because there was no way she was ever believing in love again—it hurt way too much.

As evening darkened, she came out onto the shore and walked along the lonely dock. Further down the beach, the older children were at a singalong campfire. The younger ones were already in bed. She had lost her hunger and sat dull-eyed and vacant, staring across the gray-blue water to where the spirits drifted, their bodies glowing as they slept. What good were they—they never did anything, never sent her any messages, never spoke. What did they matter, what did anything matter? A hot tear slid down her cheek.

Sudden laughter came dancing out of the night trees. Five girls were coming down the path to the beach, their pale bodies wrapped in towels. Whispering and giggling, they stepped onto the dock.

Adrien felt a clutch at her throat. There wasn't enough room. What should she do—jump off the dock and watch from the water? Trapped in indecision, she scooted to one side and watched as they paused a foot from her, looking at one another.

"Now!" said Roberta, and all five dropped their towels. The moon lit every curve of their naked bodies as they stood shifting hesitantly on the dock.

"This is embarrassing," said Cath.

"No, it isn't." Roberta stretched out her arms. "It's glorious. The air's kissing my skin everywhere."

"I'm going in." Nat took several running steps and dove into the water, followed by Sherry's cannonball. Cath slipped in slowly, Roberta dropped off the edge, standing at attention. The last girl spun and dropped in backwards. Her face was frightened—the water closed over her head like dread and she came up fighting.

"Over here, Debbie," Roberta called. The girl swam out to her and was promptly ducked. "This feels so cool," sang Roberta. "I hate swimsuits. I'm never wearing one again."

The girls splashed and dog-paddled, floated on their backs and counted stars. Even Debbie seemed to relax, losing her look of fear.

Adrien couldn't stop watching their bodies. Their breasts floated gently in the water, their buttocks flashed in the darkness, going under, surfacing again. It was like a dance, the girls playing with the water, letting it touch and stroke them—some kind of utter freedom she had never imagined.

"What d'you think Erin is doing now?" Roberta called as she came paddling toward the dock.

"D'you mean what is she doing, or exactly what is she doing?" Nat called back.

Roberta giggled. "It's a good thing she doesn't know we sneak out while she's gone. Otherwise she'd have to be responsible and lonely all night in her bed."

"Thinking about Peter Pecker," sang Sherry.

Suddenly Roberta surfaced directly in front of Adrien, grasped the dock firmly and hauled herself out of the water. Twisting, she planted her butt exactly where Adrien was sitting, then leaned back, shaking the water out of her hair. Adrien sat rigid and disbelieving as the other girl continued to lean back on her hands, her legs splayed, splashing one foot in the water. Gradually, Adrien let herself relax. She could feel the other girl's body all around her own. Roberta was humming. Tiny vibrations rippled through her chest, there was the steady thud of her heart, the quiet lift and fall of her rib cage as she breathed, the cool slide of water over her foot. Adrien could even feel the air shift along the girl's wet skin. She had never known skin could feel so alive—it was like an entire forest rippling in a slow breeze. If only she could read Roberta's thoughts ... Adrien let her head fall back and saw the vast panorama of the night sky, its wild sprinkling of stars, the shadowy green glimmer of the Northern Lights.

"We should stop wearing bras," Roberta declared suddenly, leaning forward. "Ditch all our underwear."

"Like women's libbers?" called Sherry.

"We'll string them up the flagpole," declared Nat, swimming small circles.

"Bras are different," Cath said. "Everyone can tell you're not leaned on the railing, watching her approach.

"Paul called for you," she said. "Several times. Wants you to call him back. You can use the office phone."

"Could I borrow a quarter?" Adrien couldn't have this conversation in front of anyone, especially her aunt. Digging a quarter out of her jeans, Aunt Erin dropped it over the rail. Then she gave Adrien the phone number and went back into the office. Adrien headed for the camp's pay phone and punched the number in shakily.

"Hello?" Paul's voice sounded husky, raw.

"Hi."

"Adrien?"

"Yeah."

He paused and she waited, teetering on the edge of everything.

"It's not that I don't like you," he said. "I like you a lot more than Leanne. It's just that everything's like fire, burning so vivid. Everything I want's on the other side of my birthday. I've got to wait until then, okay?"

"I don't know when your birthday is," she said. "My brain could blow. I could be dead by then."

"No," he said quickly. "You're always there. I dream it."

She thought of the five girls, the joy in their bodies, the laughter they carried everywhere. The way they had dropped their towels. "I'm going to kiss you tomorrow," she said, and listened to his breathing quicken.

"Adrien—"

"Paul, did you *make* Leanne do it?"

"No!" he exploded.

"Then maybe *she* was the one who made the mistake,"

wearing one. You jiggle."

"You're supposed to jiggle," said Roberta, jerking her s
ders so her breasts swung. "We'll have a Jiggle Revolution."

Giggling, Sherry cupped her own breasts and jiggled th
Soon the other girls were following suit. Then Nat dove underu
ter and the Jiggle Revolution ended.

"I hate the way my boobs move when I walk," said Debbie, up
to her neck in water. "I always try to keep them, y'know, solid, like
a guy's chest, so I don't get embarrassed."

"Plastic Barbie tits," agreed Sherry.

"It's embarrassing, the way guys stare," said Cath.

"They're just jealous," said Roberta. "I'm going to stick my
tits out like a wooden mermaid on a ship's prow." Lifting herself
up on her hands, she dropped back into the water.

The scene began to fade. *No,* Adrien thought desperately. *Please don't go.* She hung on to what she could see—
pale white flashes that glowed eerily in the water. Then she
realized she was seeing two sets of girls, their bodies and
their spirits, swimming together like dolphins, diving and
surfacing, weaving around each other in a kind of caress.
They never quite touched—the girls seemed unaware of
the spirits, feeling their presence as a loose shifting joy.

This time the scene faded completely, leaving Adrien
staring at the empty water. Above her, the sky was still
light and a few stars had come out. Down the beach, the
campfire was breaking up. She felt solidly, ravenously hungry and stood slowly, feeling every fiber in her body, a forest rippling quietly in her skin. As she climbed the path
and crossed the lawn, she wondered who would take pity
and feed her this late. Her aunt came out of the office and

said Adrien. "Maybe she didn't know enough to say no."

"Maybe. I think I knew that, though. I just had my head in some fucked-up place."

"Okay, so you both fucked up," she said. "It didn't kill you. Or her."

"Yeah, okay," he said quietly.

"And—" She thought of the girls again and swallowed. "Well, I'm here *now*."

"Yeah." He was smiling, she could hear it. "You sure are."

"Will you kiss me back?" she asked hoarsely. "I've never kissed anyone. I don't know how to do it."

He gave a quiet laugh. "You catch on quick. Don't worry."

A soft easy breath lifted through her. "I won't then," she said. "Worry."

"This is going to be one long sweaty night," he said. "See you tomorrow."

"Yeah," she whispered. "See you tomorrow."

She hung up the phone and stood in the booth's white light, listening to her heart beat. It was a promise repeating itself, becoming truer each time it spoke.

twelve

The master cabin was a one-bedroom apartment, equipped with a kitchenette and a washroom. The main room held a sofa, stereo and bookshelf at one end, the tiny kitchen, a card table and several stacking chairs at the other. There was no TV in sight. Telling Adrien to sit down, Aunt Erin got some cold meatloaf, mustard and milk out of the fridge and fixed her a sandwich.

"Drink the milk," she said. "Good for you."

As Adrien ate, her aunt sat across the table, toying with a piece of bread. Adrien waited for a barrage of questions about missing supper and wandering the woods all evening, but there was no interrogation, no advice. Maybe her aunt felt she had none to give.

"Paul and I," Adrien said into the silence, "had a sort

of not-fight fight, but I guess we're okay now."

"Weren't at flag lowering tonight." Aunt Erin watched her own fingers tear at the bread. Her shoulders were slumped and her breathing seemed labored. Adrien hesitated, then decided to open a door.

"Aunt Erin, have you ever been in love?"

Her aunt's eyes widened. She dropped her face into her hands and rubbed it. "Yes," she said quietly.

Adrien watched her carefully. "It's confusing, isn't it?"

"Yes," her aunt said again, not looking up.

"But I think I like it."

"Paul's a boy of honor," said her aunt. "Couldn't find a better young man. Just remember your whole life's ahead of you."

Like you did? Adrien thought, but asked, "Could I use your toilet?"

The washroom was tiny, just a shower stall, toilet and sink. The walls seemed thin, and she wondered how cold the room got in winter. Aunt Erin was a true Spartan. While the toilet flushed, Adrien opened the medicine cabinet. While she was sick, she had seen a biographer explain to a TV talk show host that whenever he interviewed Hollywood stars in their homes, he always checked their medicine cabinets because that was where people kept their secrets. Immediately, Adrien found what she was looking for—two prescription bottles, one for sleeping pills and the other for Prozac. Aunt Erin was on anti-depressants. If she was mixing it with sleeping medication, it was no wonder she hadn't heard her niece yelling from the Petting Zoo. Closing the medicine cabinet, Adrien scanned the washroom for more details. A bottle of blond hair dye stood in the shower stall. So, her aunt was keeping the gray out of her hair, pretending to stay young. Living in the past. When Adrien came out of the washroom, Aunt Erin was still at the table, picking at the piece of bread.

"Aunt Erin," Adrien said. "Those girls in the photograph—who were they?"

"Just a cabin of girls I counseled."

"But why d'you keep their picture where you can always see it?"

"Something I need to do."

Adrien didn't know what to tell her—the girls had been more alive than anyone she knew? They had been happy, their bodies had hummed with a music most people never heard? Her aunt already knew that.

"I'm glad you asked me here this summer," she said slowly. "I'm learning."

Her aunt looked up, a quick gladness in her face. "Good. Now, time for bed. Your mother'd be having a fit."

The knock came around 1 AM, waking them both. "Whaaaaaaat?" Darcie moaned into her pillow. "I thought I was going to get some sleeeeeeep."

The door opened and hall light shone into the cabin bedroom. Adrien squinted at the dark shape leaning in the brightly lit doorway. "Darcie, you coming?"

"No."

"Why not?"

"I want to sleeeeeeep."

There was a pause. "The rest of us want to sleeeeeeep too."

"Then go to bed."

"They'll get us," said a second dark shape, "if we're alone in our own rooms."

The doorway was now crowded with girls. Darcie sighed and sat up. "Geeeeeeez," she groaned. "Bring your mattresses in and put them on the floor."

"We'll have to sleep double," said someone.

"C'mon, Grouch," said Darcie. "If I have to sleep with someone, it's going to be you."

Adrien scooted across and climbed into Darcie's bed. As the other girls brought in their mattresses, she plumped her pillow, then snuggled and burrowed until she was comfortably warm and happy, surrounded by the scent of Darcie's perfume.

"Hey," complained her roommate. "I didn't say I wanted to play teddy bears. And do you mind? I'm plastered against the wall."

"I like your bed." Adrien had the giggles.

"Well, you can like my bed facing the other way. Then there'll be *some* room for me."

Adrien obligingly turned to face the room, and Darcie got comfortable behind her. The other girls were doing the same, shifting and sighing in their beds. "What d'you think they'll do to us?" asked someone nervously.

"What can they do to eight girls in one room?" Darcie was scornful.

"Well, you know all those school shootings—"

"Connor doesn't have a gun," Darcie said emphatically.

"Besides, he's not the loner type. Mass murderers are loners. Ever see him alone? He's a wild partier."

"Anyway," said Adrien, "we've got Robin Hood."

"Hey, Darcie!" said someone. "Tomorrow, bring your bow and arrow to bed."

"You're not sleeping in here tomorrow!" exclaimed Darcie.

"Oh yes we are," chorused the other girls.

Darcie muttered into her pillow. Gradually the girls' breathing evened out until it seemed an extension of the night sighing through the trees.

"Spart, you awake?"

Darcie's arm lifted and came around her, patting her shoulder. "See what you started? Freedom. A revolution."

"One of the guy counselors talked to me this morning. He said a lot of staff are mad about the cage thing."

"I think Connor's going to fizzle like a popped balloon."

"Weird, eh? Sure didn't feel like it a couple of days ago."

Darcie patted her shoulder again. "People just need an example, Grouch. You're a hero."

Adrien was getting happier and happier. "I like all of us sleeping in one room."

"I sure hope no one snores."

"Y'know, Spart, I could die in this bed before morning," Adrien teased sleepily.

"You're giving me the willies."

"If I did, I'd shit my pants."

"Honest, Grouch. How'm I supposed to sleep, thinking—"

Adrien fell asleep.

At flag raising, Connor stood poker-stiff, staring straight ahead. When Bunter spoke to him in the breakfast line, he gave terse replies, then fell back into his thoughts. Whispers traveled as stories were traded about last night. It sounded as if more than half the staff had opted for sleep, and the campfire had been a desultory affair. Initially cautious, staff standing close to Connor began to relax. Their invisible leashes were falling off. When jokes were told, the laughter came out differently, less like a chorus. By lunch, everyone had stopped shooting glances in his direction, as if asking for permission to act like individuals. Darcie's prediction was coming true—Connor was fizzling like a popped balloon.

Adrien felt like an over-pumped balloon. She had seen Paul briefly at 8:30, and they had agreed to meet at four. All day, she thought about the expression on his face. Was she being stupid, or had he smiled enough? Had he really touched her hand, or had she just imagined it? Last night on the phone, his voice had been so raw, and this morning when he first saw her, he had taken one quick breath as if he had suddenly run short of air.

Finally, the last cabin came through Tuck'n Tack and she was free. Paul helped her close, then waited while she took in the till. As they walked into the woods, he took her good hand. Heat pulsed between their palms. One of the last mayflies sat in his hair, catching the light in its wings, but she left it there.

"What did you dream about last night?" she asked.

"You," he said, squeezing her hand.

"Did I die?"

"No," was all he said, and a warm flush crept up both their faces. He stopped in the clearing he had taken her to for their first smoke, and started to pull out his pack of cigarettes. She shook her head.

"You quit?"

"I don't feel like it right now."

Shoving the pack nervously into his pocket, he removed his lumber jacket and dropped it under a tree. "Okay, um, let's see," he said, looking around. "Usually, before you get to the, uh, kissing part, you do something else—bowling, biking, dancing. I thought maybe we could dance."

"Dance?" Adrien hadn't been to a school dance since grade eight. She couldn't remember a thing about dancing.

"It's easy." Now that she looked petrified, he looked a little less so. "C'mere," he grinned. When she didn't move, he stepped close, slid one arm around her waist and took her hand. Hesitantly, she put her other hand on his shoulder. All over, her skin was coming alive with new feelings. Paul spoke into her ear.

"I'll be the music. All we have to do is shuffle." He started to hum low in his throat. "Got any favorites?"

She was getting the giggles again. "The bullfrog one. Jeremiah with the wine."

"That's an oldie. I don't know all the words, but I know the tune." His voice wavered huskily, and it helped that he couldn't sing well. With Paul, things were raw-edged and honest—nothing had to be perfect. She could feel the vibrations of his voice in his throat and chest and his breath ruffled her hair. Gradually, her tension slid away, she closed her eyes and let her body follow his. When he finished singing about Jeremiah, he started another oldie, one she recognized but couldn't name. Opening her eyes, she watched his mouth. It was so close. When was it going to happen? When were they finally going to kiss?

He opened his eyes. "Okay, enough dancing." He looked around again. "I want this to be the best first kiss in the history of mankind."

"Paul, the suspense is killing me."

"You'll live." He pulled her to a tree and they sat with their backs to it. Carefully he took her damaged hand and traced Darcie's bandage. Her heart began to thud.

"So, uh, what d'you think camels look like when they're kissing?" he asked casually.

She saw it, and a shout of laughter burst out of her.

"Snakes?" he added.

Giggles bounced around her insides. "Walruses," she snorted.

Paul grinned. "Anteaters with their snaky little tongues." He plucked a stem of seed grass. "Hold still."

The laughter had changed her whole body. She felt like water, fluid and sparkling, and smiled as he touched the grass tip to her lower lip. He drifted it across and a sweet tickle sent itself everywhere through her. He did it again.

"Oh," she whispered. "That's incredible."

He traced the grass across her cheek, her throat. Then he leaned closer and kissed her chin. "Hey," he said. "I thought you were going to kiss me."

She had never imagined it could be like this—talking, laughing, *playing*—as if the entire purpose was just to make each other happy. Taking the seed grass, she traced it gently across his mouth. Eyes closed, Paul sat leaning against the tree, his body giving the tiniest shudder each time she tickled his lips with the grass. Her skin seemed to be humming, as if her body had become a kind of music, and she felt as if she could spend the rest of her life touching his mouth. His lips were the color of a ripe peach. Dropping the grass, she brushed her lips across his once, like a whisper. Paul moaned, and she touched her mouth full to his. His lips were soft and moved in small ripples, so they were kissing endless tiny kisses, her body full of soft bursting questions: *How will this feel? How will this make him feel?* Each question asked the next. She wanted to know so much. She felt as if she was discovering the reason her body lived. Finally Paul pulled her face into his neck and they sat together, hearts pounding, letting their breathing slow.

"Thank you," she whispered.

"For what?"

"For thinking about it first."

"I've been thinking about it from the first minute I saw you." He tugged on her hair. "But, uh, Adrien? I'm real close to splitting my jeans, okay?"

Realizing what he meant, she sat up. His face was flushed, his eyes almost closed. A heavy heat blew through her, heat that was almost pain, heat she wasn't yet ready for. Reluctantly, she got to her feet. The clearing was dusty with late-afternoon light. She stretched her arms and drifted in a slow circle.

"Adrien."

She stopped and looked at him. The world still spun slightly, and at its center stood Paul, staring past her. She turned. The green-gold air was full of slight vibrations. There was an opening, she was sure she could feel an opening to some other place pulsing mid-air in front of her. She stretched out a hand to touch it. The pulsing felt like music. She wanted to hear it.

"No!" Paul pulled her back, wrapping his arms tightly around her. She felt dazed, distant, her head full of strange light. The violence of his heartbeats thudded through them both.

"Never do that," he whispered. "They were reaching for you."

His fear ran around them in circles. She yawned sleepily and waited for it to subside.

"Promise you won't do that again," he said, letting her go. "Never reach for them. If they want you, they'll take hold and pull you through."

"All right," she said, but she couldn't understand his fear. It had felt so beautiful, like a dream from which she was just waking. She touched Paul's mouth, and he sighed.

"Just think," he said. "Life could go on like this, day after day after day."

thirteen

Adrien was restless. It was evening, everyone on staff was involved with pro-
grammed activities except her, and all she
could think about was Paul. Leaving the
cabin, she drifted toward the lake. As usual,
the spirits were a soft glow, floating on the water's surface. *Wait a minute*, Adrien thought, her pulse
quickening. *They're floating just under the surface, not on it.
The way I do in my dreams.* The waves blurred their glowing
outlines, and she realized she had seen the spirits awake
several times only—twice when the weather had been
stormy, and yesterday, when they had joined the girls to
swim in the lake. They seemed to spend most of their time
sleeping. What did they dream about—the brief week they
had been alive at Camp Lakeshore? Was that why she kept

seeing the five girls—the sleeping spirits were sending her
their memories? But why her? No one else seemed to experience their dreams, not even Paul. Did Aunt Erin?

She crossed to Prairie Sky and leaned against an outer
wall, swatting mosquitoes. A group of eight-year-olds went
by on a nature walk, and shrieks from a game of Capture
the Flag echoed through the woods. Then she heard Nat's
voice, coming from inside the cabin.

"If you tell, we'll kill you."

*She moved to a window and peered in. The interior light was
on and she could see eight girls facing off in two groups—five on
one side, three on the other.*

*"You don't scare me, Nat," said one of the three. "I'm still
telling."*

"But you'll get Erin in trouble," Debbie said pleadingly.

*"She should get in trouble." The girl crossed her arms defen-
sively. "She's supposed to be here at night, looking after us. And
you're not supposed to be out there, running around."*

*"Why not?" Sherry stepped forward, her hands on her hips,
and the three girls shuffled backwards, bumping into each other.*

"Because it's not safe," blustered one of the three.

"What's not safe?" scoffed Nat. "The moon? The trees?"

"What if a man saw you?"

*"Here at camp?" demanded Nat. "Anyway, what's one guy
going to do to all of us?"*

*Roberta stood closest to the window, pulling nervously at her
hair. Cath and Debbie sat on a nearby bunk, their gazes darting
from Nat to the three girls. Debbie chewed her nails. Sherry and
Nat leaned forward in full battle position, glaring.*

"I'll find out where you live," Nat threatened. "I'll track you

down. I'll—"

"Why don't you come with us?" Roberta interrupted. "We never said you couldn't come."

"I don't want to go out in the dark," said one of the three. "And you're not allowed. You're breaking the rules. Erin's letting you and she's a bad counselor."

"She is not." Enraged, Sherry shoved her face into the other girl's. "She's in love."

"Well, she's not supposed to be," the girl said flatly.

"She doesn't know we go out," protested Cath. "It's not her fault. We sneak out after she leaves."

"You wouldn't even know she goes out," said Roberta, "except we woke you last night by accident."

"I bet you sneak out to meet the boys," said the girl farthest from Sherry, her eyes narrowed, her arms also crossed.

"No," Debbie said quickly. "We do stuff on our own."

"You were skinny-dipping," the same girl accused.

A tiny smile crossed Nat's face. "How long did you watch?" The other girl froze, and Nat closed in.

"Did you like watching us skinny-dip, Lesley?"

"I just heard you and wanted to see what you were doing." Lesley was losing ground rapidly. Her eyes faltered and she began to turn away.

"I think you liked it," Nat hissed. "Lesley the Lez. If you tell anyone about Erin or us being out at night, I'll tell everyone you spied on us because you like girls."

"We didn't spy on you," said one of the others, trying to bolster Lesley. "You could've been in trouble or something."

"No one'll believe that after the story we tell about you three." Nat was calm, tasting victory.

"I'm with Nat." Sherry smiled, twisting her ponytail. "We'll tell everyone, right, Debbie?"

"Right," said Debbie.

"Right, Cath?"

"Right," agreed Cath.

"What about you, Robi?"

When Roberta finally nodded, the air changed. The three girls stared at her, then moved apart. From this point on, anything they did together would be suspect—talking, laughing, even looking at each other. Nat had come up with the perfect accusation.

"Only a lez would want to stop Erin from seeing her boyfriend," Nat said with a satisfied smile.

The scene vanished, leaving Adrien on tiptoe, stiff from straining to see in. She was about to let go of the window ledge when another scene took shape. The three girls were lying silent in their bunks and Roberta stood in the center of the dark cabin, holding a flashlight.

"I don't think you're lezzes," she said. "Anyway, who cares if you are? It's all just love, isn't it?"

"It's dirty and it's a lie," said one of the girls.

Roberta hesitated. "I'm sorry Nat made you feel bad. She was really scared that you'd tell on Erin. Erin's ... the best counselor I ever had. She's just the best. And she's in love. Haven't you ever been in love? Mad-crazy for someone? I can tell you how it feels— like the grass, sky and air are whispering and touching each other. You're so happy, you can hardly breathe. Everything's soft and warm, and you want to lie down and roll like a kaleidoscope, so everything mixes together and your whole body's spinning while you think about the one you love." Roberta's voice wobbled, but she kept going. "That's what Erin's feeling. She spends all day and *evening trying to ignore it and be the best counselor in the world for you and me, so I think we can let her have an hour with her boyfriend while we're asleep."*

The three girls continued to lie in silence, their backs to her. "Well?" Roberta asked uncertainly, wiping her eyes. "Aren't you going to say something?"

"Will you make Nat and Sherry promise not to lie about us?" came a muffled voice. Roberta wasn't the only one crying.

"I'll talk to them," Roberta said quickly. "They were just scared. Honest."

"They're mean," said another voice.

"I won't tell on Erin," said the third.

"You won't?" Roberta swung the flashlight at her. The girl rolled over and blinked in the light. It was Lesley. She shook her head.

"No matter what," she said. "I promise."

"What about you, Patty?" Roberta aimed the flashlight at another girl.

"All right," came her reluctant voice.

"No matter what?" Roberta probed.

"No matter what," Patty sighed.

"Joanne?" Roberta lit up the third girl.

"I'll think about it."

Roberta knew she had won. A smile flooded her face and she jumped several times, bouncing light all over the cabin. "Oh, I love you guys. Thank you, thank you. I'll make it up to you, I promise."

Adrien sagged against the side of the cabin. *No matter what.* Roberta, Sherry, Nat, Cath, Debbie, Lesley, Patty and Joanne—chance had thrown these eight girls together with Erin Wood twenty years ago, and five of them had died. If the three girls had talked, the five would be alive today, but they had all believed in love. Love was the most precious thing. It brought the body alive—she could feel it now, just as Roberta had described it, a kaleidoscope that rolled and whispered and hummed in her skin.

There were too many questions without answers. Adrien was so tired, she could hardly hold up her head. Returning to the cabin, she was about to crawl into bed when she encountered two strange pillows. Without another thought, she turned toward Darcie's bed, burrowed into the smell of her own pillow and fell deeply asleep.

She woke, surrounded by the sleeping of girls. Their breathing was deep and even, placid as the lake when the air was still. Emerald light streamed through the window above Darcie's bed, shifting with slow leaves. Everything floated on a deep calm.

She was still wearing her clothes and realized she hadn't woken when the others came in last night. They must have tiptoed down the hall, then crawled quietly over the mattresses on the floor so they wouldn't wake her. Adrien drifted with these thoughts, turning and slipping through them like a skinny dipper. This was what it felt like when people cared about you—the air and water, earth and sky belonged to you; there was no difference between walking, swimming or flying; everywhere you went you were home.

Darcie's eyes opened.

"Morning, Spart," whispered Adrien.

"So you didn't die during the night?"

"Nope."

"You didn't shit your pants?"

"Nope."

"Well, that's a relief. Did Connor come in last night?"

"Not that I noticed."

"I guess that's what matters." She sat up and stretched. "I slept all night. I feel like a new woman."

"Thanks for not waking me up."

Darcie leaned against the wall and smiled. "You were hogging the bed, but you looked like an angel sleeping there, so I decided not to bug you."

The nine-year-old squirt who had lost her boombox to Aunt Erin's rules was wearing a red Camp Lakeshore T-shirt. Adrien smiled as she watched the small girl stand in silent adoration next to Aunt Erin, who was dressed in a blue Camp Lakeshore T-shirt. Above their heads, the flag rose into the wind, rippling its brilliant red and white, and early-morning voices croaked into "O Canada," gradually gaining strength. Another day at Camp Lakeshore had begun.

Breakfast was pancakes and bacon. Adrien was absolutely positive she had never been this hungry. Her first plateful dove down her throat, and she joined the line for seconds. When she returned to the table, Aunt Erin was sitting in her seat, face drawn and tired, talking to Guy.

"Not feeling well. Going to lie down. Maurice is at Ranch Camp for the day. Take over for me, would you?"

"Sure, Erin." Guy nodded quietly. "I know the schedule. Don't worry about a thing."

"I'll handle the office," Gwen added quickly.

As Aunt Erin stood, she noticed Adrien next to her, holding a plate heaped with pancakes. A faint smile lit her eyes and she placed a hand briefly on her niece's shoulder. Then she walked out.

"You were right," Gwen said to Guy. "Lucky you memorized the schedule yesterday."

"Right about what?" asked Adrien, sitting down.

"First week of camp," Guy said easily. "Erin gets overstressed about mid-week. Then she's over it and the rest of the summer goes fine."

Adrien didn't buy it. Professional camp staff stressed out in mid-August, not the third day of July. She was no longer hungry and pushed her plate away. "Is she going to a doctor?"

"She'll lie down for the day. Tomorrow she'll be fine."

"After 1:37?"

Guy gave her a confused look and Adrien decided not to pursue it. "Never mind," she said. "My blood vessels are weak today," and she got up to shovel her plateful of food into the garbage.

Paul was early. She stood waiting outside the office as he coasted to a stop in front of her. Immediately, he leaned in for a kiss. She giggled with relief, and they managed several warm sloppy ones before a shrill whistle cut them off. They pulled apart to see Guy giving them a ferocious glare.

"Now there'll be none of that while I'm in charge," he declared. "No romantic fraternizing, none at all."

"You're in charge?" Paul grinned. "Get real."

"For the day," Guy said, swaggering. "And you, scum of the earth, are helping me put in supports for the Wishing Tree."

"Aunt Erin's sick," explained Adrien.

Paul's face went quiet and he disappeared into his thoughts. "I'll lock my bike," he said, turning away.

"Would someone please tell me what's going on?" Adrien cried in frustration, looking at Guy. She knew Paul wouldn't tell her anything, but Guy's face also closed.

"It's your aunt's business," he said, heading off to meet with the maintenance crew.

By mid-morning, the sky had clouded over and a wind picked up. Children still wanted their Mars Bars and Nibs, but she also sold a few sweatshirts. At her fifteen-minute break she headed to the kitchen. Maybe the hairnets would give her some answers.

They were frenetically busy, running from boiling pots to hot ovens to countertops, all the while maintaining a constant barrage of non-English. "Excuse me," Adrien bellowed from the doorway.

The hairnets turned en masse and smiled. "It's Adrien!" one of them exclaimed. "The girl who wants to grow up to be a cook."

"Become a lawyer," said another. "Better pay."

"Better shoes," said the third. "Oh, my aching feet."

"Could I ask you a question?" asked Adrien.

"Sure, sure," they chorused and waited.

"What language are you speaking when it's not English?"

They looked at each other, surprised. "Ukrainian, dear," said the nearest one.

"How d'you say please in Ukrainian?"

Now they looked dumbfounded.

"*Proshoo*," one said quickly.

"No, no, no," said another. "Say it slower or she'll never remember. My son forgets every day and I've been telling him for years. *Proshoo*, dear," she enunciated clearly.

"*Proshoo*," repeated Adrien.

"She has it!" they exclaimed simultaneously.

"Could someone *proshoo* tell me what's going on with my aunt?" asked Adrien.

The hairnets broke into a volley of Ukrainian, shaking their heads at each other, then turned back to their pots. Adrien knew the signs. There was no point in pushing this one any further.

"Well, could you tell me when Paul Marchand's birthday is, *proshoo*?" she asked loudly.

The smiles came back. "We've ordered the cake. Such a nice cake. Sixteen candles. He'll need a big kiss, *proshoo*."

Adrien flushed but held their eyes determinedly. "What day, *exactly*?"

"It's a secret," they grinned. "Practice that pucker. Make it good for him."

It was tough to keep smiling for the seven-year-olds, even Tamai's group. Fortunately no one noticed her mood, even Aunt Erin's fan-for-life, who came through at 10:50.

"I see you're wearing a very ugly T-shirt today," Adrien said, placing the requested Caramilk bar on the counter.

"It's not so bad," conceded the girl, pulling it out from

her chest and assessing it.

"Looks better upside down?"

The girl flashed her a grin.

"You're doing great with the flag," Adrien told her.

The girl took the Caramilk bar and stood a moment, smiling at her. "I like it here."

"Me too," said Adrien.

Darcie appeared behind the girl, waving something. "I got mail!"

"How come you're not at the range?"

"It's raining. Haven't you noticed?"

"Just spitting. Robin Hood wouldn't let a few drops of water get him down."

"Robin Hood didn't have to teach archery to giggling eleven-year-old girls," scowled Darcie. She hung around as two more cabins came through, then helped close the store for lunch. Adrien carried the till into the office, her roommate at her heels. "Now, finally," said Darcie. "I can show you." She pulled a stack of photos out of a mail-order envelope. "Remember that picture I took of you and your aunt last week? I had two copies made. Here's yours."

Setting down the till, Adrien gave the photograph a casual glance and her mouth dropped. Darcie had captured them standing on the porch, leaning over the rail and looking down into the camera. Both seemed caught off guard, between expressions, somewhere within themselves. Except for differences in age and hair color, they could have been the same person.

Darcie laughed and elbowed her. "You're as gorgeous as she is, Grouch. Didn't you ever notice?"

Gwen got up from her desk and leaned over Adrien's shoulder, nodding without surprise. "Like mother and daughter, aren't they?"

"Sisters," said Darcie. "I'll get another copy made for your aunt."

"Make it for me," Adrien said suddenly. "I'll take her this one."

Gwen put an arm around her. "My guess is she'd like it today."

"That's what I thought," Adrien said.

Gwen's eyes were thoughtful. "How about now, Grouch?"

Adrien paused at the top of the stairs to the master cabin, pressed her forehead against the screen door and listened to the muffled crying that came from inside. She was about to step into the eye of the storm that whirled around everyone at this camp, the invisible mysterious storm no one would acknowledge. Without knocking, she opened the door and entered. The crying came from the bedroom, where her aunt lay on the bed, her face shoved into a pillow to keep herself quiet, her body moving in waves of grief.

"Aunt Erin?"

Her aunt lifted a startled face and stared at Adrien as if she didn't recognize her. Her cheeks were blotchy, her eyes swollen. She reached for a box of Kleenex and blew her nose, then lay down again, burying her face in the pillow. Adrien stepped into the silence, walked to the bed and sat down.

"I brought you something." She laid the photograph

next to the pillow. "Please look."

Slowly her aunt turned and saw the picture. She picked it up and held it close to her face. "That's amazing," she whispered.

"I like looking like you," Adrien said.

Her aunt's eyes faltered.

"I like being like you," Adrien added.

Her aunt gave a short wry laugh. "True, isn't it? Two peas in a pod."

"The pod's okay too."

Her aunt sighed. "Haven't been a good aunt. It's just this week. Things'll get better. Take you out for supper next week, just the two of us."

"Sure."

"I'll put this picture on my wall," her aunt added. "Next to my desk."

"Please put the other one away," Adrien said quietly. "In a photo album, where it belongs."

Her aunt breathed in sharply, then pulled the picture of the eight girls from under her pillow and laid it between them. The air pulsed with the unspoken.

"They look like they were very happy," said Adrien. "These five." She touched their faces gently. "They look happier than most people ever get to be. So do you."

"Yes," her aunt said faintly.

Adrien knew she had to respect her aunt's wall of silence. "Well, I think they loved you very much. They wouldn't want you to be unhappy, like you are now."

Her aunt lay without speaking, looking at the two photographs.

"Neither do I," added Adrien.

A few tears slid down her aunt's cheek.

"Can I bring you some lunch?"

"I'm not hungry," said her aunt.

"Yes, you are," said Adrien. "I'm going to get you some lunch right now."

She left the room quickly, took the outside steps in one jump and hit the ground running. Minutes later, she returned with a plate piled high with macaroni and coleslaw. "Drink the milk," she said, setting a full glass on the night table. "Good for you."

Her aunt sat up. "Never forget a word I say, do you?"

"No."

Her aunt smiled faintly. "Have to watch my step." She reached for the fork and began to eat. "I am hungry."

"You eat every single bite," Adrien said softly. "I love you, Erin Wood."

The words hovered between them like insect wings, flickering in a gold-green downshaft of light. Then Adrien slipped out of her aunt's startled stare and headed for the cabin's front door, which stood wide open to the storm clouds building over the lake.

fourteen

When the whine of a chainsaw tore through the late afternoon, Adrien understood immediately. Ignoring a cabin of eleven-year-old boys who were arguing about the difference between Coke and Pepsi, she climbed over the Tuck'n Tack counter, pushed through their astonished faces and took off for the Wishing Tree. The rain had let up; she flew through the still-dripping trees unaware of the looks campers were giving her, of Tamai calling her name. The chainsaw whine cut deeper into her head, split her brain into a white grinding heat, and the screaming of wood filled her. She could feel the groan of a great gleaming spirit tilt, lean, begin its fall toward earth. With it went the wishes, the broken-hearted questing wishes, the whispering hearts. Filled with their falling, dizzy with it, Adrien burst into the clearing and spotted Guy bent over a fallen Wishing Tree. She launched herself. There was the long shock of bodies hitting ground, then the two of them struggling in the wet grass.

Abruptly, the metallic whine cut off. Paul leaned over them, holding the chainsaw. "Let her go, Guy."

"Are you crazy? She went for me!" Guy had Adrien pinned and was staring down at her, his eyes bugging. "She's totally lost her friggin' mind!"

"You're cutting down that tree because Aunt Erin's sick," Adrien yelled, still fighting. "She wouldn't let you do it. That tree is sacred. You're killing the wishes of children. You're cutting down their hearts."

Guy's face changed. "Grouch," he said into her face. "Listen to me, Grouch. Hey, Adrien!"

She stopped struggling.

"We're cutting the *fallen* half," Guy said dramatically. "Not the standing part. We've attached guide ropes, see? Take a look."

Cautiously, she turned her head. Five yellow support ropes ran from the standing trunk into the ground.

"Can I let you up now, or are you still going to kill me?" asked Guy. Shamefaced, she nodded and he released her, groaning as he straightened. "Where'd you learn to tackle—the Roughriders? Geez, I wasn't even cutting the damn thing. Why'd you go for me?"

"I saw you first." Adrien was soaked and her body felt battered. Paul gave her a hand and she stood, hugging herself. "You can't do anything to the fallen part," she insisted, her teeth chattering. "It's not dead yet."

"It will be soon." Guy reached for the chainsaw.

"No!" Adrien yelled, stepping in front of him. "Its soul is still in there. You'll murder it."

"It can wait, Guy," said Paul.

Guy looked from one of them to the other, shaking his head. "This has got to be one of the craziest moments of my sweet life," he muttered. "All right, put some warning flags around it. You know where they are, Paul?"

"I'll do it right away," Paul promised.

"I would've done this last week," Guy said, "but Erin kept putting me off. She's as crazy as you are."

Giving Adrien one last incredulous look, he left. Adrien walked to the tree and knelt by the fallen half. Not much had been removed, a few branches. She put both hands on the charred bark, sent her wish deep inside and waited, but there was nothing. And then there was. A delicate tingling passed from the fallen trunk into her hands, up her arms and into her chest. She was filled with a shimmering emerald light, and singing was in the air.

It was night. A crescent moon held the center of the sky above the clearing. Five girls dressed in cotton nighties walked through the trees, holding hands and singing. Adrien continued kneeling as they approached, watching Roberta lead the girls toward her. Sherry was second in line, her long red hair a wild tangle to her waist, then Cath, Debbie and last of all Nat, in an oversized Snoopy T-shirt. The girls circled the Wishing Tree, Roberta and Nat joined hands, and the five began to sway. Their voices changed, going deep into their throats. The sound was muffled, half-buried, as if they had gone down into themselves and were struggling to find something. They began to writhe in pain—Adrien could see their hurt as the girls' eyes closed and their faces lifted toward the tree's whispering leaves, sadness pouring from their mouths. It was the same sadness she felt within herself, constant, never letting go. She stood and stepped into their circle. The girls didn't stop writhing, but room was made for her—she felt Roberta and Nat take her hands. Adrien's head fell back and she let her own sadness take her completely; her body swayed and twisted with theirs, her voice a corkscrew of grief. She didn't know why she was crying, only that grief was a song to be sung, part of the beauty of the night, and her body craved it, became more lovely as the song was released. As the girls danced and sang, their music passed into the Wishing Tree, rose along the glow of its bark into the dark whispering leaves. Then it was over, the girls' sorrow released, their faces shining with joy. Watching the peace on Sherry's face, Adrien wished that just once, this girl's mother could have seen her daughter like this.

"Now we'll make our wishes!" cried Roberta, coming out of the moment of quiet. "Bums up!"

Giggles bubbled as the girls turned their backs to the tree, flipped up their nighties and pressed their bare bums to the trunk. Amid cries of glee, they danced around the clearing, breasts jiggling, arms waving, the tree in a slow dark laugh above them.

Adrien returned to a late Wednesday afternoon to find herself standing under the Wishing Tree, the clouds above her opening onto a clear blue sky. She turned to Paul, her face radiant.

"Adrien," he whispered, and she wondered what he saw— places opening around her head, angels reaching through?

"Did you see them?" she asked. "The girls, here around the tree."

"Just you," he said. "Singing."

She reached for him, wanting the warmth of closeness. "Everything came together," she said into his neck. "Happiness and sadness, crying and laughter, the night and the light. Everything touched, and now it's the same heart beating. It used to be war, opposites fighting, but not anymore. D'you know what I mean?"

"You were singing the kind of song where you let everything go," he whispered, pulling her tighter. "What if it's you? What if you die instead of me?"

"No." She was certain. "It's not like that. It's not a trade-off. It's each of us, making our own way."

"Oh god." He covered his face. "My birthday's tomorrow and I'm not ready. I don't know enough—when it'll happen or how. If I'm going to die or if you will. I thought I could figure it out and beat it, but I can't. What'm I supposed to do?"

"It's your birthday," she said. "Somehow you'll know."

"What if I'm wrong?"

"You won't be. And I'll be there too—you dreamed it." They held onto each other.

"Make a wish," she said. "Touch the tree and wish."

"I'm touching you," said Paul. "That's my wish."

He left, not knowing whether to stay or leave, and she stood in the middle of the road, watching the wings that glistened on his back as he rode away. She ate supper in a dull exhaustion, then crawled into Darcie's bed, sleep closing like water over her head. When she woke it was dark, rain fell steadily outside, the calm even breathing of girls surrounded her.

Darcie's clock read 1:22. Heart quickening, Adrien sat up. Her clothing had dried and stuck to her skin. Her shoes were lost somewhere in the corners of the room. She crept over the sleeping girls, down the hall and out into the night.

It was raining; the moon glimmered faintly through fast-blowing clouds. She reached the lawn and began to run, headed for the lake. At the end of the dock she could see a single canoe slipping into the water, carrying five giggling fifteen-year-old girls. Their night held the same rain, but Adrien could see the girls as clearly as if she was in the overloaded canoe with them—Roberta at the prow, Nat at the stern, Sherry, Cath and Debbie between them.

They were laughing at Nat's lousy steering, but she got the knack quickly and the canoe headed straight toward the deep. Roberta handed her paddle to Cath, draped both her legs over the prow and took off her nightie, imitating a mermaid figurehead. Then, without warning, Sherry stood mid-canoe and jumped a cannonball off one side. Crying out, Nat leaned forward to balance the rocking canoe, but it tipped, throwing everyone into the water. The heavy frame crashed down on top of the girls, knocking their heads, pulling them under. The canoe quickly filled with water and sank. Three girls surfaced as the first lightning flickered low across the horizon. A storm was building quickly, kicking up waves around them.

Adrien reached the ridge and ran down onto the beach. The girls were crying out, their voices calling to her. How could she reach them? She couldn't paddle a canoe by herself in a storm.

"Well, if it isn't little Wood."

She hadn't noticed the lone figure sitting on the dock, and slid to a halt as Connor stood and beckoned. "Come to make pax?" he asked. "Come for that canoe ride?"

So the midnight campfires were a complete bust and the waterfront coordinator was out here, sulking in the rain. She hesitated, then stepped onto the dock. Connor was always a reason to walk the other way, but she had to get closer to the girls, see their last moments. If she couldn't bear witness to the very end, everything would be in vain. She would fail the girls and their spirits, and the reason they had sent her their dreams would be lost. She was part of this, she knew that. But how? And why?

"I was just heading out." Connor's wet hair was plastered to his head.

"In the rain?"

"I'm an excellent canoeist." His face remained expressionless and he stood as he had before, one hand stretched toward her. Again, lightning flickered across the lake, thunder rumbled, waves rose and crashed. The girls' cries were growing faint. What choice did she have? She had to hurry. Already, two were gone.

"Okay." She began to walk toward Connor.

The night woke up. There was the slam of the master cabin door and the sound of Aunt Erin's voice calling Adrien's name as she came running across the lawn, yellow jacket flapping.

Connor hadn't seen the camp director yet. He stepped into the canoe. "C'mon, Angel."

"Adrien," she said automatically, staring out at the lake.

"No!" called her aunt's faraway voice. "Not her too. You can't have her too."

Farther out, beyond the drowning girls, the spirits were coming awake. Rising half out of the water, their arms reached toward Aunt Erin in a pleading gesture.

"All right," screamed Aunt Erin, bending forward. "I let you go. I set you free."

The spirits lifted, unfolding from their dreams, and as they rose from the water a pair of wings spread out from each one of them, huge with strength. *Dreaming for two decades*, Adrien thought, staring in wonder. *Aunt Erin's finally let go of them and now they can fly—toward what?*

The loud whine of a dirt bike broke into her consciousness. She turned to see Paul riding at full speed through the rain, passing Aunt Erin as he headed straight for the ridge.

Only two girls were still alive, treading water in the storm. As they reached for each other, a bolt of lightning forked gracefully above them, its tiny fingers skipping down to touch the water's surface. Without a sound, the girls disappeared beneath the waves and the five spirits lifted free, wings flickering wildly. At the same moment, Paul crested the ridge, pulling his bike into a high arc. Instinctively, Adrien knew that he must have woken from a dream of her and Connor on the dock, that he had come to save her. The bike's arc was perfect— it would have carried Paul to the edge of the dock where he could have cut Connor off easily, but then a hard shove from behind sent Adrien reeling forward. Helpless, she stumbled directly into the bike's path, forcing Paul to kick free mid-air, the movement twisting and upending his body. The bike crashed heavily into the water and Paul began to fall headfirst toward the dock.

The spirits were a line of light flowing faster than thought toward shore. Adrien reached toward them, begging, and the first one entered her, passing through every molecule, traveling every blood vessel, lifting upward into her brain. The next spirit came into her, and the next. She heard each one singing in a clear girl's voice, each spirit *was* voice, the spirits a river of song touching her through and through. The girls had been joy, and so were their spirits. Death hadn't changed this.

Adrien lifted her arms toward Paul, sending the spirits upward into him. They passed through his body, their giant wings outstretched, catching and cradling him, slowing his fall as they sent their pulse of joy deep into the fibers of his being. Leaving him, they flew on toward Aunt Erin, outlining her five times with their wings. Then a place opened in the air, so vivid with leaping colors that Adrien cried out in astonishment. Hands reached from there to here, the five spirits passed through, the place closed itself to human eyes, and was gone.

Paul was still falling, slowed by the spirits' passage and the wings of hope that flickered on his back. Thinking to catch him on her shoulder, Adrien stepped forward. He landed, she stumbled beneath his weight, and there was nothing to catch her as she fell, carrying him, to the dock.

fifteen

She could feel someone breathing on her lips and opened heavy eyes to see Paul's face hovering just above her own. "Adrien," he whispered. She tried to lift her hand to touch his mouth, but it wouldn't move. Her arm was strapped to her chest. Then she noticed one of Paul's arms was also wrapped in a sling.

"You've been sleeping for hours," he said. "We're in the hospital. You dislocated your shoulder and broke your collarbone. I broke two ribs and dislocated my shoulder too, but we're alive. I'm alive, you're alive."

"Happy birthday." Relief made her giddy, lifted her high above the white hospital room. He kissed her nose and she came back down.

"You saved me," he said quietly. "I would've landed on

my head."

"Well, I knew you were coming to save me." Adrien tried to joke, but her voice wobbled. "Besides, I like your head."

"But with your aneurysm—it could've set something off, couldn't it?"

"It was your birthday, but you still got out of bed to come rescue me."

"I woke up around quarter to one and I kept seeing Connor's face," Paul said tiredly. "His ugly face, and something about the dock. I didn't like his eyes—nothing there, no feeling. I just knew you were there."

"The girls were out on the lake. I could see them drowning. Connor said he'd take me for a canoe ride. I thought I could get closer."

"He shoved you, didn't he? I thought I had a clear landing, but then you were there, stumbling like you'd been pushed."

"Yeah," said Adrien slowly.

"He took off last night," said Paul. "Guy told me all his stuff was packed and gone this morning. Must've cleared out while everyone was out there watching the ambulance pick us up." His voice broke and he started kissing her. She closed her eyes and followed his warm soft lips across her face, trying to catch them with her mouth. She wanted to kiss his mouth forever.

"Would you look at that!" Guy's cheerful voice declared from the doorway. "They're both in straightjackets and they're still going at it!"

Paul straightened quickly, and Adrien saw Guy and Aunt Erin enter the room, followed by her parents.

"Supposed to be in bed, Paul," Aunt Erin scolded with a smile, but Adrien's father was frowning and clearing his throat. Then Adrien noticed Paul wasn't wearing a pajama top because of his bulky arm support. That would be more than enough to set her father off, not to mention the kissing.

"Get you sitting up," Aunt Erin said quickly, adjusting the bed. "Guy, take that boy back to his room."

Paul gave Adrien one last grin before leaving. Then her mother was leaning over her, patting her hair, whispering and kissing her. "I'm fine, Mom," Adrien said, but without her old impatience. She would have reached for her mother, but her right arm was strapped to her chest and the left gave off pains whenever she moved.

"You're lucky," her father said gruffly, tucking the blankets around her. "Out running around in the rain. Going out in canoes at night. That boy in here when you should be resting."

"Shh, Greg. She's not ten anymore," said her mother.

"That boy almost caused the death of her!"

"No," protested Adrien. "He saved me. He knew I was in trouble and he was coming to save me. He has a sixth sense, Dad."

"Paul's a boy of honor," Aunt Erin said firmly. "You need a reference, I'd put my life in his hands."

Adrien's father grumbled his way toward a chair and sat down heavily. Her mother and Aunt Erin pulled up two more chairs. Everyone perched on the edge of a nervous silence. Taking a deep breath, Adrien faced the half-circle of adults around her bed. "So, when can I go back to camp?" she asked. Watching her parents' faces fall, she knew she was in for a fight. "I can still do my job," she said quickly. "I only need one hand to work in Tuck'n Tack. Paul's the one out of a job."

Aunt Erin cracked a thin smile. "Put him in Tuck'n Tack with you. Be your other hand."

Adrien burst into a laugh but was silenced by her parents' expressions. Her father cleared his throat. "You're coming home with us. Doctor McKeown wants to keep you in for observation another day or so, to see if this has affected your brain. Then we'll drive you home."

"It's just my shoulder, Dad!" Adrien wailed. "My blood vessels are fine."

"Doctor's orders," her father said firmly.

"But I want to go back to camp." The tears were sudden and shattering. "Mom? Please? I'm different there. I like being me when I'm there."

Her mother swallowed hard, then looked at her sister-in-law. "Are any of the guest cabins free?"

"Stay with me," Aunt Erin said immediately. "You get the bed, I get the couch."

"And I stay in my cabin?" Adrien pleaded. "I won't do anything strenuous, I promise. You can even come into Tuck'n Tack and watch me work. I'll sit in your lap." She watched her father melt. "Daddy, please? I'm happy there."

He blinked ferociously. "All that kissing. Very strenuous."

"We don't kiss much," Adrien said. "I just woke up and he was happy I was all right."

Another loud throat clearing erupted. "Yes, I noticed that."

How could she convince him she needed to be at camp?

She had to dig deeper into the truth. Maybe he could meet her there.

"I had a dream," she began, "just before I woke up. I could see my body. It was dead and the eyes were open. They were blue like they're supposed to be, and they didn't blink or move. There was no breath, no heartbeat. The mouth wasn't smiling, it wasn't crying, it was just ended. I touched the face and it was cold. The skin was sort of gray and hard to move. Like rubber, I guess."

The three adults breathed as if air was slow raw pain.

"And then I saw my spirit," Adrien said, "floating just above my body. I reached out and touched it. It felt ... like the sound of a thousand singing bells. Happy bells—the high tinkling ones and the low booming ones. Full of triumph. It felt like laughter."

Her mother was leaning forward, her mouth open as if she wanted to swallow Adrien's words and take them deep into herself. Their eyes met, completely open doors.

"Mom," Adrien whispered.

Her mother nodded, then looked at Aunt Erin. "We'll stay with you, Erin. Thanks for your offer."

"I dunno," began her father.

"We'll stay with Erin," her mother repeated firmly.

Paul was released that evening while she was asleep, but she talked to him on the phone the next morning. It was a long wait until Saturday when the short round doctor that had been shining lights in her eyes and ordering brain scans agreed to let her out. "Make sure she takes it easy," he admonished, "but happiness is the best medicine. This is a happy camper you've got here."

The drive back to camp was quiet. Adrien floated on a peace that was heavy like dreaming, peace that dreamed like water. When they pulled into the parking lot, it was early evening. The first week of campers had gone home that afternoon and the grounds were quiet. She called Paul and he said his mother would drive him over to see her in the morning.

"You still dreaming?" she asked suddenly.

"Yeah, I'm dreaming," he said slowly.

"Not about dying?"

"It's kind of X-rated, these days. Don't tell your dad."

"I don't tell Dad about *those* kinds of dreams."

"I hope they're about me," said Paul.

"Uh-huh," mumbled Adrien. Blushing on the phone— how embarrassing. "So you have to dream about me too, okay?"

"Uh-huh," said Paul.

"Promise?"

"Cross my heart, hope to—" He paused, then added, "Live."

Adrien kissed her parents good night and let them hold her the way they needed to. Years passed between them, two years of pain and fear, wrapped in love, finally understood. Then she gave her aunt a one-arm hug.

"Hey," Adrien asked softly. "Did the spirits say anything to you when they passed through?"

Her aunt let out a quick groan of air. "Something I've

been waiting to hear for a long time."

"Music?" asked Adrien. "Singing?"

Her aunt's eyes brimmed with tears. "They used to sing like that all the time."

"They still are," said Adrien. "Did you know you've got wings on your back?"

"What?" Aunt Erin gave her a confused look.

"Dream wings," said Adrien. "They suit you."

Darcie tucked her into bed, full of advice on how to sleep with a broken collarbone. Except for the two of them, the cabin was empty. Other staff were using the free evening to visit family and friends.

"But not me!" said Darcie. "Oh no—I had to welcome my best bud back. It's been boring here without you, Grouch. No one complaining, pointing out all my problems, rebelling over the tiniest itsy-bitsy thing."

"You're a sucker for punishment," said Adrien. "Did I ever tell you that I don't like the color of your nail polish?"

"What's the matter with fucshia?"

"It doesn't match Camp Lakeshore T-shirts."

"Blue, green or red?" Darcie demanded, making a face.

"You should try harder to fit in, Spart," said Adrien. "Be a better role model. Don't you realize your nails flash in the sunlight when you're holding a bow? It's very dramatic. The kids'll get all confused if the colors are wrong."

"Let me see," said Darcie, rummaging through the bottles of nail polish on the dresser. "I've got a bottle of forest green."

"Emerald green?"

"Nope, none of that."

"Forest, then," said Adrien, falling asleep.

She woke in the earliest part of morning and lay watching the emerald leaves play at the window. The light was calling to her—she understood without words. Standing, she crossed to Darcie's bed and kissed her softly on the cheek.

"That you, Grouch?" Darcie asked sleepily.

"Sweet dreams," Adrien whispered, and her roommate drifted back to sleep. She left the cabin and walked into the woods, huge with the scent of spruce. All about her the day was beginning, flowers showing their colors, birds opening their beaks with song. Beneath her feet, the earth seemed to be humming, restless with its own music. Leaving the trees, she crossed the lawn, her bare feet leaving tracks in the dew. Ahead, the horizon was vast with pink and amber clouds. She passed the clearing where the Wishing Tree stood, and an empty Prairie Sky. Then she was at the ridge. Here, she turned to look back at the place that had taught her how much she was loved. For a moment, she saw each dear one breathing easy in sleep, and sent a wish into their dreams. Then she descended the path that led to the beach. A late mayfly settled onto her bare arm and she let it ride as she walked across the cool sand. The lake was quiet, the storm that had been building for twenty years gone now.

She sat on the sand and stared out at the water. Two weeks ago, when she had first arrived with her parents, she had come to the lake immediately, as if called. It had seemed so familiar, as if she had spent the past two years here, dreaming a deep heavy dream. Now, she had come fully awake.

She could feel the wings on her back; they stretched wide on either side, flickering with colors she had never seen—deeper than black, brighter than white. The mayfly lifted off her arm, flying away. She watched it, wondering how long she would fly—two days? Twenty years? But wasn't that a question everyone wondered? No one knew when death would come, or how. A long clean breath lifted through her, and Adrien realized she was normal. Maybe the greatest tragedy wasn't how you died, but how you lived your life. So many people lived in full fear of dying. For her, that had changed. She had seen the spirits pass through; when her death came she would know how to follow. The same joy lived on both sides. It would carry her through.

Adrien stood, took two steps toward the great dreaming water. The gentlest of light touched her brain and she reached with her strong arm, welcoming the horizon.

"I'm alive!" she shouted, and her voice flew across the lake.